COMING OF THE DURSTUROCK

COMING OF THE DURSTUROCK

JENNIFER FYRE

HYPATIA PRESS

Published by Hypatia Press in the United Kingdom in 2025

ISBN: 978-1-83919-689-8

www.hypatiapress.org

To everyone who has dared to stand up to authority and question the status quo. Let evidence prosper.

Chapter One

The odenpom's long shaggy hair caught on the wooden tines of the comb. Cara grunted and yanked the brush harder, but the hair refused to yield.

"Just my luck," she muttered, releasing the brush and staring at the odenpom accusingly. Early morning rays of sunlight broke over the horizon and highlighted the brownish hairs on the odenpom's back, matching the golden-brown strands hanging in front of Cara's blue eyes.

"It's too early for this. Why can't you just keep your hair untangled?"

The odenpom swung its large head around, big golden eyes staring innocently back at Cara. Long soft ears swayed gently back and forth on either side of its face, hanging well past its chin.

Cara sighed and pushed her hair out of her face. "Look at me, talking to an odenpom. I'm losing it."

The odenpom swung its head away and resumed its morning breakfast, tearing apart a large clump of weeds nearby. Cara leaned back and observed the animal sourly. It wasn't the odenpom's fault, really. It was her father's. Ever since he gave her guardianship of three odenpom, her mornings were filled with grooming, cleaning, feeding, and fatigue. But she had to get up early to make it to school on time, and even earlier to care for the animals.

"Creator my foot," Cara grumbled, reaching forward to grab the handle of the brush again. "The Creator should be able to take care of his own messes."

The door to the side of the feed shed slammed shut with a loud bang as an apprentice priest stepped into the yard. Cara yelped and leapt back from the odenpom, withdrawing her hand just in time. A large and very solid boulder lay in its place, with the wooden handle of her brush sticking out of its side.

Cara jumped to her feet and glared across the yard.

"You dumb baki!" she shouted. "What's the matter with you?"

The apprentice priest frowned. "I was just coming out for my morning chores…"

Cara snorted. "Could you be any louder?!"

The apprentice priest shrugged. "I'll be more careful next time." He turned his back on her and shuffled to the far corner of the field, dragging a large bucket of dried grasses for the scutneys grazing by the fence.

Cara glared at his back for a few moments before slowly turning back to the boulder. She slowly kneeled by its side and began whispering soothingly.

"Everything's okay, you don't have to worry. The field is safe and you won't come to any harm."

The boulder shuddered slightly.

"Really, everything's safe now. I promise." She reached out her hand and gently stroked the top of the boulder. "Nothing's going to hurt you."

With another slight shudder, the boulder began to change. The cold gray stone melted away into long shaggy brown fur, and the golden eyes of the odenpom blinked dolefully at Cara. She reached forward and tentatively tugged the handle of the wooden brush. The comb snapped in half, the mangled and twisted remains of the tines deeply embedded in the odenpom's hair.

Cara sighed and set to work removing the wooden scraps from the odenpom's coat. "You have to be half mad to create a creature like this," she muttered, picking out several tines with her fingers. When she finally finished, she stood and patted the odenpom's head before striding toward the feed shed. Several odenpom lumbered across her path, keeping a wary eye on her as she passed. Cara yawned as she glanced at the herd. Her father had said that caring for the animals would teach her responsibility and respect for the Creator's creatures. But all it had done so far was make her tired and grumpy.

She reached the feed shed and slipped inside, dumping the remains of the comb into a waste bin by the entrance. The morning light shone through the cracks in the walls, highlighting the dusty floor in odd stripes. Cara squinted through the dim lighting, searching the walls for another brush.

"Cara!" a voice softly called from the yard. Cara sighed and shuffled out of the feed shed, following the voice.

"Cara!" the voice repeated, slightly louder this time.

"Over here," she called out in response, stepping into the yard. Her father stood in the doorway of the back entrance of the church, his long white robes hanging just above the muddy grass of the field.

He looked at her reproachfully. "Cara, you're going to be late for school. You should have left several minutes ago."

Cara groaned and looked at the rising sun. It was just cresting the horizon, the early morning rays highlighting the muddy grass with golden hues.

"Where's your Penlet? You need to get moving!"

Cara sighed heavily and trudged towards the back door. She slipped past her father, ignoring his critical eye, and grabbed the small copy of the Penlet from her room, stuffing the thick text under her armpit. Before her father could reprimand her again, she rushed out the front door, hurrying along the dirt road that led toward the center of town.

It was a long walk to school – half an hour if you walked quickly. That was no problem for Cara. The more distance she put in between her and her father the happier she would be. It was a pain to take care of odenpom in the morning, but at least the animals didn't criticize her every thought and action. At least the animals didn't make her study the Penlet every day. At least the animals listened to her.

It wasn't long before she caught up to some other students on the road – two children a little younger than her thirteen years. Both carried small Penlets beneath their arms, their shiny covers gleaming in the sunlight. They reluctantly made space for Cara, carefully averting their eyes from hers. Cara smirked with grim satisfaction. As much as she disliked her father, it was

4

sometimes nice to have the High Priest as a dad. Many of the children were too intimidated to speak with her, but she was okay with that. Most of the time she didn't want to speak to them either.

The small group walked in silence the rest of the way to the school. Long flat fields of crops stretched away on either side of the straight dusty road, dotted with tiny farmhouses in the distance. The village was quite large considering its population; a little over three hundred inhabitants were spread over the large farms and sprawling fields. Plenty of crops were visible, but animals were a rare sight on farms. All animals were considered gifts from the Creator, and were therefore in the care of the church.

A spatter of rain hit Cara squarely on the head. She winced and glanced upwards as small showers of rain fell from the sky below it. A small flock of iraa birds winged past, their long, iridescent feathers glinting in the sunlight as the rain fell below them, creating a multitude of miniature rainbow refractions. One of the children snickered, but quickly fell silent when Cara glared at him. She wiped away some of the water trickling down her face, and adjusted the book under her arm. Iraa birds were certainly useful during a drought, but Cara thought they were a nuisance at any other time.

Finally a cluster of structures rose above the swaying crops. The road widened to a large circular area, surrounded by several old but well-kept buildings. Even from a distance Cara could recognize the pointed roof of the blacksmith's shop and the rounded top to the inn. Travelers were very rare, but the inn was a common place for villagers to meet and share a meal. The schoolhouse, a single-story building with weathered wooden walls, was set slightly apart from the actual village center. Cara groaned at the sight of the flaking red paint and the gathering children. The only thing she hated more than listening to her father's lectures was going to school. She dragged her feet through the dirt on the road, falling behind the other children, and reluctantly stepped into the classroom after everyone else.

Forty-eight students, from ages eight to sixteen, sat calmly at their desks in a large, bright, airy room. Paper rustled across the room as students leafed through their Penlets, opening to yesterday's lesson for a quick review. Cara grudgingly slouched into a chair near the back, dropping her Penlet loudly on the desk in front of her. A fellow student, a boy slightly younger than Cara, gave her a reproachful look. Cara rolled her eyes and slouched down further in her chair. She didn't care if the Penlet was sacred. To her it was just another set of lectures.

"Good morning, class!" The teacher, a middle-aged man with short black hair and a severe face, strode into the class-room.

"Good morning, Mr. Baynor," the class chorused. Cara mumbled along, indifferent.

"Could everyone please stand for The Creator's Prayer."

Chairs scraped back as the students slowly got to their feet. Everyone made the sign of the Creator, touching their fingertips together then tapping them to their foreheads. Finally voices swelled from the classroom, joining together in prayer.

"The Creator and his glory shine upon us all. Let His mercy light our way, His wisdom guide our hearts, and His love save our souls. His path is the one true path of salvation and redemption to deliver us from evil."

There was a brief moment of silence as the teacher nodded his head, then the shuffle of chairs and feet filled the room as everyone settled into their chairs. Mr. Baynor slowly opened his eyes, looked around the room with a critical gaze, then picked up his elaborately embossed Penlet.

"Today we'll be continuing our lesson on the Sacred Caves," he began, flipping through the gilded pages with care. "Does anyone remember which rituals are performed there?"

The boy sitting next to Cara raised his hand.

"Yes, Peter?"

Peter straightened up in his seat, clearing his throat. "The Initiation Ceremony, the Ritual of Thanks, and the Remembrance."

"And what is the Remembrance?"

"Fourteen days of solitude, ending with a two day fast. Each day represents a year, symbolizing the time our ancestors used the caves as shelter from the Dursturock."

The teacher smiled, his thin lips stretching across his normally stern face. "Very good, Peter. With any luck, someday a few of you will be able to visit the caves and perform this ceremony yourself."

Cara snorted a little too loudly. Mr. Baynor frowned, deep furrows appearing in his brow as he glared at Cara.

"Do you find that funny, Chandra?"

The entire class turned to look at her, anticipating the usual argument. Cara frowned at the use of her formal name. She sat up a little straighter and lifted her chin defiantly. "I don't see why anyone wants to visit the caves."

The teacher's frown deepened. "You cannot visit the caves unless you are a confirmed priest. This is an honor that all of you should strive…"

"But what if I don't want to be a priest?"

The teacher carefully closed his Penlet and placed it on his desk before giving Cara a long and calculating stare. "It's true that most people will not be given that honor, but you should work towards it nonetheless. Being a priest means serving the Creator in everything you do."

Cara shrugged. "I don't see why we have to dedicate so much of our time and energy into serving Him."

Peter, sitting to Cara's right, let out a small gasp at her comment. The teacher raised one eyebrow, drumming his fingers on his Penlet. "The Creator cares for us and protects us every day. Our families, our homes, the animals – we owe them all to the Creator and His generosity. And all he asks in return is for us to learn about Him and follow His way."

Cara frowned. "He doesn't protect us. He allows bad things to happen all the time! He knows exactly what will happen *and* he has the ability to stop it, so why doesn't he?"

The class seemed to be holding its breath, anxiously glancing back and forth at Cara and the teacher. The teacher gave her a wary look. "You must trust that the Creator has a greater plan – one that you may not have the capacity to understand. Now back to the lesson…"

Cara snorted, her anger getting the best of her. "Last week the Torin's new baby girl died from fever. How does that factor in to the Creator's greater plan?"

The teacher straightened, glaring at Cara angrily. "Don't take that tone with me, Cara. You must show respect for the Creator."

"That's stupid," Cara shot back. "How can I show respect for someone who would let a baby die for some dumb plan? Someone that I've never even seen!"

Mr. Baynor slammed his fist down on his desk. "Quiet Cara! You've gone too far this time. Leave the classroom immediately, and remain outside until you're ready to behave yourself."

Cara sat still for a moment, then jumped to her feet and stalked across the room. Astounded eyes followed her as she yanked open the door and left the classroom.

A cool breeze greeted her, lifting her golden-brown hair off her shoulders. Bright sunlight beamed down through clear blue skies, but Cara didn't notice any of it. She stormed down the dirt road and veered off to the right, entering a field of tall grasses. Fuming, she strode through the plants, letting their papery stalks scrape at her arms and legs. After a few minutes, she began to slow down, her fury turning into resentment.

"Stupid baki Baynor," she muttered to herself. She kicked at the base of some nearby grass, and sat down abruptly. "It's not fair." She clenched and unclenched her fists. "I hate learning about the Creator, and I hate getting punished for asking questions." She slammed her fist on the ground, and yelped at the jolt of pain that raced up her arm. She sat for a few minutes, cradling her hand, and gazed at the fields around her. Eventually she reached out and picked a long strand of grass, twirling it between her finger and thumb. *No one understands, not even my father...*she groaned at the thought of the High Priest. If the teacher reported the fight to her father, she would never hear the end of it. *I went too far this time. I should've kept my mouth shut.*

Cara continued to twirl the strand of grass, but something odd was happening with her arm. She frowned, concentrating on her hand, and noticed that her movements were very slow and exaggerated. Every twirl of the grass took nearly twice as long as it should have. She cocked her head and it also moved in slow motion, as if there were some force slowing down time. Then she gasped, "dunbee!"

She looked around, albeit slowly, and noticed a small brown tail vanish in between two stalks of grass. It was a nest of dunbee! They were small, mousy creatures, with long torsos and small pointed faces. It took several dozen of them to slow down time to this extent – a single dunbee had virtually no effect.

Cara slowly rose to her feet, now fully aware of the strange sensation of moving in slow motion. She began to follow the pack, but they were far too fast for her. They slipped through the grasses, unaffected by the time field, and quickly scurried out of sight. Within a few moments, Cara began to move normally again. The majority of the dunbee must have passed out of range. Suddenly a quick blur caught her eye. A lone dunbee, far behind the pack, darted through a clump of grass at her foot. In a flash, Cara pounced on the grass and cupped her hands over it. The sound of angry squeaking quickly reached her ears. She carefully lifted her hands, taking care not to release the animal, and then opened them a small crack to see.

Curled in the palm of her hand was a tiny dunbee, shivering in fright. Cara slowly lowered it into a fold of her shirt and grabbed some grains from the top of a nearby strand of grass. She slowly placed the grains in front of the little dunbee and waited for it to move. The dunbee slowly opened a beady black eye, looking around for an escape route. Spying the grains, it quickly snatched up the food and stuffed the grains into its cheeks. Cara grinned at the sight.

An idea suddenly blossomed in her head. She smirked, tossed in another handful of grains, and then quickly covered the dunbee in a fold of her shirt. She slowly stood up and set off for the school, striding back towards the peaked roof visible through the tops of the grasses. As she walked she could feel the dunbee trembling with fright while cramming food into its overstuffed mouth.

Finally she emerged from the grass field, stepping onto the hard dusty road. She walked briskly towards the school, and adjusted her hands innocently in front of her shirt to cover the bulge where the little dunbee sat feasting. She entered the room, and the class instantly grew silent. Mr. Baynor set down his Penlet and gave Cara a reproachful look.

"Are you ready to behave, Cara?"

Cara nodded innocently, averting her eyes and staring at her feet.

Mr. Baynor continued to stare at her, hesitating at her sudden obedience. "I trust there will be no more outbursts?"

"No sir," Cara said, rather truthfully.

Mr. Baynor stroked his chin, and then nodded slowly. "Good. Please sit down in your seat."

Cara repressed a grin as she shuffled over to her desk. The dunbee quietly squirmed under her hands.

The teacher cleared his throat, keeping one eye on Cara. "So, as I was saying, the Sacred Caves are considered to be the most holy location in the world. They are so holy, that only people that have dedicated their entire lives to the Creator are allowed to enter."

Cara slowly transferred the dunbee from the folds of her shirt to her palm. The little dunbee let out a tiny squeak, but it was muffled by her hands.

"The Sacred Caves have been a source of inspiration and creativity for many generations. Many writers and poets have tried to describe their beauty, but none come as close to the famous priestly poet Jean Whittemore." Mr. Baynor's eyes finally left Cara's, wandering around to observe other children in the room. "Today we will memorize his most famous work, 'Protector of the Light,' and compare it to the description of the caves from the Penlet."

Cara hunched forward and opened her hands near the ground. The startled dunbee leapt out of them and raced across the room, dashing between desks and squeaking frantically. It brushed against several legs, but by the time the students looked down, the dunbee had passed them.

"Could everyone open to page 257? As I recite the poem, make sure to…"

"AAAAIIIIIIIIIIIIEEEEEEEEEEEEEEEE!"

Chapter Two

One of the older girls, a sixteen-year-old who was graduating in a few months, leapt out of her chair and on to her desk, screaming at the top of her lungs. Mr. Baynor jumped in shock at the scream, then his brow furrowed in displeasure.

"Grayla, please sit down immediately. What is the matter…"

"AAAAAAAAAHHHHHHHHHHH!"

Two more students leapt onto their desks, yelling quite loudly. Cara spotted the little dunbee again as it darted away from the screaming students and raced down the center of the classroom, straight towards Mr. Baynor. Almost everyone could see it now, but Mr. Baynor was distracted by the class.

"Settle down! Sit down, I say! I don't know what's gotten into you all, but…"

The little dunbee scampered over his shoe, and Mr. Baynor looked down quickly. Upon seeing the dunbee he yelped and jumped back in shock, tripping over the corner of his desk and banging his elbow on the wall. In sheer terror, the little dunbee dove into the dark recess of the teacher's bag, hoping to find a place to hide. Upon seeing this, Mr. Baynor leapt back to his feet and seized his bag, slamming it against the ground with surprising force.

Cara, who had been lapsing into silent giggles during the whole affair, jumped to her feet in concern.

"Stop it!" she yelled angrily. "You're going to hurt it!"

Mr. Baynor abruptly stopped and stared at Cara.

"You…" he sputtered. "You did this."

Cara flushed red and raised her chin in defiance. "Prove it."

Mr. Baynor dropped his bag and gritted his teeth. The little dunbee raced out of the bag, squeezed into the narrow crack under the door, and raced outside to freedom.

"Come to the front of the class, right now."

Cara swallowed, pushing down the lump of fear that swelled in her chest. She slowly walked to the front of the room, passing through rows of students. Several students climbed back down from their desks, embarrassed by their outbursts. Cara reached the front of the room and stopped in front of Mr. Baynor, trying to ignore the stares of her classmates.

"Kneel."

Cara glared at Mr. Baynor, determined to resist.

"Kneel!"

Cara reluctantly knelt, dropping to the floor.

"Now pray to the Creator, and apologize for your actions."

Cara gritted her teeth.

"Now!"

She dropped her head and mumbled a prayer. "Creator, please forgive my actions on this day. I have acted wrongly and I regret my decisions."

Mr. Baynor jerked his head. "Good. Now apologize to the class."

Cara squeezed her eyes shut and forced out another apology. "I'm sorry for creating a big disturbance, and I'm sorry that I scared a lot of you."

The class silently stared at her as she slowly rose to her feet. Mr. Baynor cleared his throat, closing his eyes and regaining his composure. "Thank you, Cara. I hope you remember this the next time you feel the urge to disobey the Creator. For the rest of the day, you will read and memorize passages from the Penlet. I have several in mind that will remind you of the importance of obeying your elders."

Mr. Baynor guided her to the back of the classroom and seated her in a small desk in the corner of the room. She reluctantly took out her Penlet and began to read the passages Mr. Baynor showed her.

The rest of the school day passed in a blur. Cara could hardly read the words in front of her. She kept on reading the same line over and over as she replayed the morning's events in her mind. She began to daydream, imagining a whole herd of dunbee racing across the room and covering the evil Mr. Baynor from head to toe. She smiled at the thought.

Finally midday arrived. Mr. Baynor dismissed everyone in the class who was thirteen and under. Cara stood quickly and slammed her Penlet shut. She dreaded next year, when she would have to stay with the older students for another three hours, but for now she couldn't wait to get out of the classroom and put this horrible day behind her. She rushed for the door.

"Cara!" Mr. Baynor's sharp voice froze her in her tracks. Cara reluctantly turned around.

Mr. Baynor strode towards her, something clutched tightly in his right fist. "Cara, you were very disrespectful today. I trust you will let your father know of today's events?"

"Yes," Cara lied.

Mr. Baynor frowned, doubtful. "Of course. Nevertheless, I must give you this today, to impress upon your father the severity of your disobedience."

Mr. Baynor held out his right hand and unclenched it. In his palm lay a thick round wooden token, stained deep red. Cara's eyes narrowed, and she bit back an angry retort.

Mr. Baynor eyed her warily. "I haven't had to give a reprimand token out in several years. I hope this will be the last one for several more."

Cara slowly lifted the token out of the teacher's hand, then spun around and stalked out of the classroom. She let the door slam behind her as she rushed down the dirt pathway. Angry tears began to blur her vision. It was all so stupid. A surge of hate rushed through her veins, and she wiped away the tears on her cheeks with a vicious swipe. She hated Mr. Baynor, she hated her fellow students, she hated everyone!

She stopped suddenly and threw the reprimand token on the ground. She lifted her foot and smashed it down on the wooden surface, breaking it clean in two. She quickly knelt down, picked up the pieces, and flung them as far into the corn field as she could. She stood for a moment, panting with fury, and then strode towards her home with grim satisfaction. Her fellow classmates eyed her nervously as she passed by.

Cara easily made it home in thirty minutes – a testament to her long, angry strides. After dropping her Penlet in her room, she wandered into the main chamber of the church. She slowly began performing her chores while munching on a loaf of bread, restocking the Penlets at the end of the aisles and replacing the burned-out candles lining the thick stone walls. The monotonous work calmed her – she had been helping the priests with their chores since she was old enough to walk. Several other priests and worshipers wandered around the room, but she ignored them, oblivious to everything but her work. After finishing, she sat down in one of the pews and sighed, finally calm. She gazed around the room with fondness. Although this room represented everything she resented about the Creator and his lessons, she still found it peaceful to be in. It was quite beautiful – the carefully placed stones were carved with caring hands, soaring around her into arches and pillars surrounded by thick sturdy walls. Flickering candles lined the room, throwing dancing shadows on the richly colored tapestries that hung on most of the walls.

Cara stretched out on the church pew, lifting her legs and resting them on the seat in front of her. The room was enormous – easily the largest in the village. It was capable of holding all 300 residents, but that only happened on the Creator's Day, the first day of the new year. Cara closed her eyes and imagined the pews full of people, raising their voices in song as thick snow piled up on the window panes.

"Cara?" Her father's familiar voice drifted over the rows of pews. Cara opened her eyes, her heart sinking.

"Yes, father?"

Her father stood in the doorway of his office, a small frame to the right that led to a lofty chamber adjacent to this room. He beckoned to her.

"Come, Cara, I need to speak to you."

Cara slowly stood up, unfolding her lanky frame and sighing. Whatever this was about, it was bound to be bad.

Her father disappeared behind the door, and Cara followed. She stepped into the High Priest's office, performing the customary sign of the Creator before facing the desk. The thick carpet beneath her feet complemented the colorful tapestries on the wall, creating a cozy but luxurious appearance. To her surprise, Cara noticed two other students in the room, the same two that lived near the church. She eyed them suspiciously, but kept her mouth shut. The two students shuffled their feet nervously. They were clearly uncomfortable in her presence and they stood stiffly, keeping their eyes averted from Cara.

Cara's father cleared his throat from behind his desk. He sat erect in his chair, and nodded towards the two students. "Martha, Taylor, could you please repeat what you told me?"

The boy blinked nervously. "Yes, High Priest. Today Cara was given a reprimand token by Mr. Baynor. She smashed it on the way home and threw it into the fields."

Cara clenched her fists in anger, and shot the boy a piercing look. The boy winced and stared down at his toes.

The High Priest studied his daughter carefully. "Cara, is this true?"

Cara looked between the boy and her father. She was tempted to lie, but somehow she doubted her father would believe her. She gritted her teeth. "Yes, it's true."

Her father closed his eyes, a haggard expression on his face. "What did you do?"

She stared at him defiantly. "All I did was ask a few questions about the Creator."

Her father raised an eyebrow. "And?"

Cara shifted her eyes to the floor. "And I let a dunbee loose in the classroom."

Her father slowly rubbed his temples. "I see," he said softly, after a short pause. He opened his eyes and nodded to the two young students. "Thank you, Martha and Taylor. You may leave now."

The two students scurried out of the room, making the sign of the Creator as they shot furtive looks at Cara. The door clicked gently behind them.

Her father gestured to the chair in front of his desk. "Please sit, Cara, we have a lot to discuss."

Cara folded her arms in front of her chest. "There's nothing to talk about. I apologized at school already, and I'm not going to apologize again."

The High Priest frowned. "Sit, Cara. Please. Let's not turn this into an argument."

Cara walked to the chair and sat down stiffly.

Her father nodded. "Good. Now Cara, we have talked about your behavior before. It is simply unacceptable to criticize the Creator..."

"But I wasn't criticizing!" Cara burst out. "All I did was ask..."

"I don't care what you asked," her father interrupted. "Chances are, you were rude, you were arrogant, and you were blasphemous. I've put up with your attitude for years, but I can't ignore it any longer. You are too old for these silly outbursts, and they need to stop."

Cara sat silent for a moment, considering her options. She eyed her father critically, but her anger outweighed her caution.

"I don't believe in the Creator," she whispered, her heart fluttering nervously. She mostly said it to infuriate her father, but the words felt right as they left her lips.

The High Priest turned white as a sheet. "What...what did you say?"

Cara raised her chin and her voice. "I don't believe in the Creator," she repeated.

The High Priest stood up quickly, concern etched across his brow. "Stop it, Cara. Stop it now. You can never say that again. Ever."

Cara, who had been expecting an explosion of anger, stared at her father in puzzlement. "Why not? I spend all day learning about the Creator and His greatness, but I've never seen Him or even heard Him. Why should I believe in Him?"

"Because he is the Creator!" her father yelled. He closed his eyes, regaining his composure, and slowly sank back into his chair. "Chandra, you just don't understand. The Creator exists, and His glory is all around us. He protects us and cares for us every day, but only because we believe in Him. As a member of this village, you are expected to believe in Him too."

Cara frowned. "No."

The High Priest slammed his fist on the desk, making Cara jump. "Yes! Do you have any idea what will happen to you? Or to me? The High Priest's daughter, rejecting the Creator. I would be the laughing stock of the village! Maybe even removed from my post. And you…" he swallowed, deep concern crossing over his face. "They would cast you away from the village, away from your family. You will be exiled."

A part of Cara recognized the danger ahead, but she was too stubborn to back down now. "I don't care," she said more bravely than she felt. "I'm sick and tired of reading and praying and learning about the Creator! Mother never would have made me do this!"

A dark shadow passed over the High Priest's face. He stood up slowly, staring down at Cara threateningly. "You will believe," he intoned in his most menacing voice. "The Creator is all powerful and all knowing, and He has given us everything. The least you will do in return is give Him the respect He is due. Your mother always did the same, even when she was confused at the end."

Cara jumped to her feet, yelling right back at him. "You don't even care about me! All you care about is your stupid baki Creator!"

"Cara!" the High Priest reprimanded. "You must believe in Him. You must!"

Cara spun around and sprinted away from her father, yanking open the door and darting across the main chamber.

"Stop, Cara! Wait!" Her father's voice faded away as she darted into a side door, down a short hallway, and then into the backyard, the large field that housed all the big animals. She raced past dozens of odenpom as they turned into boulders around her, frightened by her frantic sprint. Ahead of her lay a sleeping scutney, a creature with two legs, a long neck and longer tail, covered entirely by short bristly fur. Struck by a wild idea, she swerved towards the scutney and leapt onto its back, startling the creature out of sleep. Terrified, it squawked and jumped to its feet, and with a flash of blinding light they were gone.

Chapter Three

Cara blinked, trying to clear the spots from her eyes. The scutney below her pranced to the side, curling its neck around to see the creature on its back. It stared at her accusingly, clearly dismayed that Cara had teleported along with it.

"Quit staring," Cara shot back, putting her hands on her hips. The scutney eyed her suspiciously and then, after deciding that Cara was not a threat, lowered its head to munch on some grass.

"Good," Cara huffed, as she looked around to get her bearings.

The scutney had teleported them to the top of a large grassy hill – one of the many that surrounded the valley the village was nestled in. Miles of wild grasses swayed in the wind, the green and brown blades dancing beneath a clear blue sky. Small patches of short, gnarled trees sprang up here and there, but mostly the hills were overrun by grass. She squinted and stared at the center of the valley, raising a hand to block the bright sunlight from her eyes. In the distance below her she could make out some tiny buildings. She smiled at the sight. The scutney had teleported her a dozen miles north of the village, at the least. There was no way her father could find her here.

"I'm free!" she burst out, and a peal of laughter erupted from her lips. The scutney raised its head and stared at her reproachfully before slowly sauntering across the hill, sampling various grasses as it walked. Cara sighed and relaxed, watching the scutney graze as she contentedly sat on its back. Most people knew better than to ride scutneys. Apart from it being against the rules (animals are considered gifts from the Creator and are to be cared for, not used), no one can control where the animal teleports next. On a whim the scutney could appear anywhere, dragging anyone in close proximity with it. In this case, however, Cara was glad for the spontaneity. It meant no one would know where she was, or how far she had traveled.

Cara examined the scenery around her. She had never been in the hills before, and the view was spectacular. She could see for miles in every direction, and she could even make out the distant snowy peaks of the great mountains to the north. As the evening wore on, the scutney slowly traveled down one hill and up another, and the sun slowly inched towards the horizon. It wasn't long before Cara's stomach began to growl.

Cara glanced at her stomach, and then at the sky. The sun was clearly setting now, and the air had already become a little chillier. Suddenly the idea of staying in the hills to hide from her father wasn't so funny after all. The thought of returning home, however, filled her with dread. She stubbornly sat on the scutney and tried as hard as she could to ignore the gnawing hunger in her stomach. The sun sank further in the sky, and it began to grow dark alarmingly quick. Finally, Cara cracked.

"Hey scutney, I think it's time to go home now," Cara said timidly, a little frightened at the prospect of being alone in the hills in the dark. The scutney ignored her and continued grazing.

"Hey," she called a little louder. "Home, I said. I think we should go home. Don't you think that's a lovely idea?"

The scutney ripped up another mouthful of grass, slowly chewing it between large flat teeth.

Cara frowned. There really was no way to force a scutney to teleport, but she had to try. Facing her father after the day's events would be unpleasant, but no worse than spending the night cold and hungry in a strange place.

"Home!" she shouted, kicking the scutney. "Let's go home!"

The scutney snorted and whipped its head around, baring its flat teeth at Cara and hissing. Frightened, Cara sat very still, staring into the narrowed brown eyes of the scutney.

"Sorry…" she whispered.

The scutney snorted again and slowly turned its head forward, walking in the opposite direction of the valley.

Cara was too frightened to protest. Before long the sun sank behind the hills on the west side of the valley, leaving only the stars and a thin sliver of a moon to light the hills. Cara trembled on top of the scutney and tried to ignore her fatigue, her hunger, and the cold.

"This is so stupid," she muttered angrily. "How could I have been so stupid? Why would anyone run away without provisions?"

She looked around, desperate for some sort of shelter. To her surprise, a bright light suddenly flared on the adjoining hill. She gasped, but as soon as she noticed it, the light disappeared.

"What…" she trailed off, frowning in puzzlement. Suddenly another flash of light occurred, this one dimmer but further up on the adjoining hill.

She squinted, thinking hard, and then it came to her. "Belknay!" she exclaimed, elated. "But…how?" Belknay never strayed far from humans. They were very dependent on the food the church provided them. But no one lived in the hills – everyone lived together in the valley. So how could belknay live up here?

Another flash of light twinkled merrily at her. Encouraged at the prospect of finding another human, Cara tried to gently urge the scutney into heading towards the adjoining hill. The scutney ignored her, and instead slowly sat down and lay its head down on the ground to sleep.

"Stupid scutney," Cara grumbled, dismounting from the animal's back. It opened one eye and gave her a threatening stare. Cara quickly backed away and put some distance between them before turning and striding towards the blinking hill. In less than half an hour she had clambered down the peak of her own hill and started up the slopes of the other. Even in the cool night air she began to sweat, small rivulets running down her forehead and into her eyes. All the while the pulses of light grew closer and closer.

Finally a flash of light erupted not twenty feet from her. She swerved in its direction, walking slowly so she wouldn't scare the belknay. After a few steps she noticed a gently pulsing light, only a few shades brighter than the night around her. She could just make out the belknay's two short stubby legs and thick beak. Thin fragile arms protruded from its front, and its scaly body had no tail and a rather plump, short frame. Overall, the entire animal was only as tall as Cara's knees.

"Hey," she called out softly, adding some little clicks that the priests usually used to summon belknay for feeding.

A blinding flash of light erupted from the belknay. Yelping and shielding her eyes, Cara staggered backwards and fell, rolling several feet down the hill before skidding to a stop. She rubbed her eyes and blinked fiercely, trying to keep the fleeing belknay in sight. After several moments the world slowly came back into focus, and she caught a glimpse of pulsing lights disappearing over the hill. She growled and jumped to her feet, racing up the hill after the belknay. As she grew closer to the top of the hill, she noticed a familiar sort of flickering spilling over the ledge. Cara climbed over a small shelf of rock protruding from the hill and clambered onto a plateau, and then gasped at what she saw.

A cheery roaring fire burned in a small stone fireplace, visible through a large glass window nestled in a cozy little house. Most of the cottage was built from a sturdy looking wood, with some sort of a mud paste used to fill in the cracks. A stand of small trees stood to the right of the structure, similar to the ones that dotted the hills in the area. Half a dozen belknay hopped anxiously in front of the cottage, croaking in alarming tones and pulsing with light.

Cara barely had time to wonder what a house was doing out here when the front door of the cottage swung open. An older man, thin and balding, stood resolutely in the doorframe and stared defiantly back at the night, the glow of the fire behind him outlining his frame.

"Who goes there?" he called, his voice surprisingly gruff.

Cara shrank back, but the hunger in her stomach gave her courage. She stepped forward. "My name is Chandra."

The old man frowned. "A girl? They sent a girl?" He cocked his head to the side. "Come closer, Chandra. Step into the light; let me see you."

Hesitantly Cara stepped closer to the old man into the light cast from the doorway.

The old man raised an eyebrow as he looked her over. "Whatever are you up here in the hills for?"

Cara scuffed her toe on the ground. "Well, I had a fight with my father, and I ran away."

The old man snorted. "A likely story."

Cara frowned, annoyed at the old man's tone. "I did! I jumped on a scutney and it teleported me up here into the hills. I've been wandering around all afternoon."

The old man eyed her suspiciously. "Okay, say you did run away. How did you find me here?"

"I saw the pulsing belknay, and I followed them here." She put her hands on her hips, her anger getting the better of her. "I'm cold, I'm tired, and I haven't eaten since breakfast. Are you going to help me, or should I just leave?"

The old man blinked, taken aback by her bluntness. "Well, I suppose you could stay for a little…"

"Thanks," Cara snipped, and she stalked forward into the cottage, brushing past the old man on her way.

As she stepped into the cottage, a small lithe form dropped from the ceiling in front of her face. Cara threw up her arms to protect herself, and the form quickly curled itself around her right arm.

"Hold still!" the old man barked, and with great effort Cara froze, resisting the temptation to shake off the thing and run screaming back into the night. Holding her breath, she opened her eyes and got a closer look at the thing.

It was a queechee! Its thin, lithe, serpentine form was covered with small soft scales, with four agile limbs wrapped around her arm. The long prehensile tail curled around Cara's right elbow, while its thin tapered head rested at the end of a long flexible neck. Thin transparent wings were folded tightly over its back. Overall it was rather large for a queechee – its body was as long as her forearm.

The queechee stared at Cara intently, golden irises surrounding narrowed black pupils. After a few tense moments, a strange rumbling emanated from its throat and it relaxed its grip on her forearm, nimbly climbing up her arm and perching on her shoulder. From there it looked at the old man and gave a high-pitched chirp.

The old man laughed, a coarse sort of chuckle from deep in his throat. "I reckon Cheea likes you," he commented. "I usually find her to be an excellent judge of character."

Cara swallowed nervously, trying to ignore the animal on her shoulder. "You…uh…you own a queechee?"

The old man crossed the room and sank into a large, well-worn armchair. "I wouldn't say own, exactly," he mused. "More like roommates."

Cara looked at the animal dubiously. "But, um…aren't you afraid she's going to burn your house down? They aren't exactly safe, you know. Not even the church protects them."

Much like dunbee, queechees were not considered gifts from the Creator, despite their magical talents. Queechees had a knack for breathing fire, and they had burned down more than one church in the past few centuries.

The amused look on the old man's face vanished quickly. "None of my business what the church does. Hypocrisy certainly isn't new for them."

An awkward silence followed. Cara shifted nervously on her feet, and the old man stared into the fire, his eyes far away. Suddenly a loud grumble emanated from Cara's stomach, drowning out the crackling of the flames.

The old man snapped out of his reverie and stared at Cara. "Was that your stomach?"

Cara nodded.

The old man looked at her quizzically.

"So, can I have some food?" Cara prompted.

The old man looked vaguely surprised. "Oh, yes, right. Of course, you're hungry." He rose from his chair and shuffled towards an adjoining room, presumably a small kitchen.

Cara walked across the room and sat on the floor next to the fire, extending her hands to warm them by the flames. The queechee chirped again and clambered down from her shoulder, jumping onto her lap and curling up on one of her thighs. It rested its long chin on the tip of Cara's knee, and closed its golden eyes in contentment.

Cara tore her eyes away from the strange creature and looked around the space. The cottage consisted of two rooms – a large living space and the smaller adjoining kitchen. The fireplace was the grandest thing in the room. It was carefully crafted with meticulously laid stones, with a stout chimney rising through the thatch roof. Surrounding the fireplace lay a worn armchair and a thick rug, with a small table to the side of the armchair. In the corner of the room there stood a small bed, with rumpled blankets falling to the floor.

The old man abruptly returned from the kitchen, carrying a plate laden with some sort of a grain mash and purple fruit slices. He held the plate out to Cara, but before she could reach for it the queechee raised its head. The animal snorted a short puff of bright flame onto the plate, and then lay its head back on Cara's knee.

The old man gestured for Cara to take the plate. She slowly accepted it, and the old man turned and returned to his chair. Cara hesitantly poked at the food, and found that the purple fruit slices were pleasantly warm and roasted after the queechee's fire. She took a tentative bite, and her eyes widened as the warm flavorful juices gushed onto her tongue.

"What is this?" she asked, holding up the slice of fruit.

"Junga fruit," the old man replied, a trace of a smile on his face. "It comes from the trees that grow all over these hills. They don't grow in the valley."

Cara took another bite, relishing the taste. She quickly fin-ished the fruit, and moved onto the mash, shoveling it into her mouth with her fingers in her haste. The old man stared at her, amused, as she quickly devoured the meal.

When she finished, she reluctantly placed the plate on the ground. The queechee immediately popped its head up again and jumped to the ground, licking the crumbs off of the plate with vigor.

Cara leaned back against the table and closed her eyes, satisfied now that her stomach was full. After a few minutes, she opened her eyes again and looked at the old man curiously. His eyes were also closed, and he seemed to have fallen asleep. His face was lined with many wrinkles, but upon closer examination he was not as old as he appeared. Perhaps fifty, if Cara had to guess.

The old man suddenly opened one eye, staring straight at Cara. She blushed, but maintained eye contact.

"Who are you?" she blurted out. "I mean, what's your name?"

The old man considered her for a moment. "You don't know?"

She frowned. "Should I?"

He sighed. "I guess I am getting old." He straightened himself in his chair. "My manners are getting rusty, Chandra."

"You can call me Cara," Cara said.

He smiled. "Cara it is. My name is Bakinu."

Cara repressed a snort of laughter.

The old man frowned. "What? You find my name funny?"

Cara quickly straightened out her face. "I'm sorry, I didn't mean to be rude. It's just that your name sounds a lot like baki."

"That is what I am often called."

Cara looked at him quizzically. "You're actually called baki? Why?"

32

"It's my name." The old man looked annoyed. "What's wrong with it?"

"Well," Cara began, surprised at his ignorance. "Baki is an insult. It means stupid, or dumb, or ignorant."

Bakinu looked as if he had been slapped in the face. "I see…" he said stiffly. "Of course my humiliation wouldn't end with exile."

Cara cocked her head. "Exile?"

Bakinu closed his eyes wearily. "Yes. The punishment for my crime. I was cast out from the village over thirty years ago, and I have lived here ever since."

Cara stared at him, amazed. "You've been living up here, all by yourself, for thirty years?"

Bakinu smiled sarcastically. "Almost. Every couple years or so some villagers stop by to steal my animals or light fire to my cottage. But most of the time I am alone, yes."

"Why?"

Bakinu studied Cara closely. "Because I don't believe in the Creator."

Chapter Four

Cara gasped. "You don't…"

Bakinu rolled his eyes. "Don't start with me. If you wish to leave, please do. I don't believe in Him, and there's nothing you can say or do to convince me…"

"But I don't believe in Him either! Or at least, I don't think I do…" Cara trailed off.

Bakinu looked at her sharply. "Don't play with me, Cara. I've spent many years reflecting over my decision, and I don't need any more punishment."

"I'm serious!" Cara exclaimed, leaping to her feet. The queechee jumped back from her, alarmed. "That's why I ran away from home! I had a fight with my father about the Creator, and I got so mad that I ran away and jumped on the scutney."

The old man studied her closely. "What you say is true?"

"Yes!" Cara insisted.

Bakinu allowed the hint of a smile to play on his lips. "So I'm not alone after all. You are also an atheist."

"A what?"

"An atheist. A non-believer. One who denies the existence of the Creator because there is no evidence, no proof. Either that or you're agnostic."

"Agnostic?"

"A fence sitter. One who isn't sure if the Creator exists or not, so plays it safe by saying they don't really know since there is no proof either way. Which are you?"

"Um, I'm not sure really. I guess an atheist," said Cara, sitting back down on the ground next to the queechee. "It's hard to believe in something you've never seen. Every time I ask my father or my teacher about the Creator the answers never make sense. I just don't understand why He would make the world the way it is."

The old man smirked. "It was the same with me. Eventually my questions got noticed by the High Priest, and shortly after I was exiled from the village. It was only a month before my nineteenth birthday."

Cara flushed a deep red. "The High Priest exiled you?" She thought quickly, doing the math in her head. Her father had been High Priest for her entire life, but he couldn't have been in the same position over thirty years ago, elsewise he would have been around ten when he was elected.

Bakinu shrugged. "Who else? When theistic views are challenged, it is the responsibility of the church to cast the dissenters out. Take my word for it, Cara. Don't let the priests find out about your disbelief. It's not worth it in the end."

"But, um…" Cara swallowed nervously. "The High Priest already knows I don't believe in the Creator."

The old man's eyes widened in alarm. "He knows? Your father reported you?"

Cara looked down at her feet. "Well, actually…the High Priest is my father." She continued to stare at the ground, too embarrassed to look Bakinu in the eye. The flames from the fireplace threw shadows across the rough wooden planks on the floor and onto her toes.

After a brief moment of silence, Bakinu threw back his head and let loose a huge guffaw. His laugh was surprisingly pleasing, a deep hearty rumble that emerged from his chest and spilled out from his lips with force. Cara looked up, alarmed, and then grinned at his mirth.

"You…your…you…" he gasped. "Your father is the High Priest! A High Priest with an atheist for a daughter!" He wiped tears from his eyes. "Oh, ho ho ho, the irony!"

The queechee jumped onto the arm of the chair, interested in the old man's laughter, and cautiously extended her neck to sniff Bakinu curiously. Slowly the old man gained control over himself and took a deep breath, clutching his stomach.

"It's been so long since I've laughed, it actually hurts," he grimaced, still smiling through his pain.

Cara smiled in return, an idea suddenly blossoming through her head. "Let me join you out here. If you can live in exile, then so can I."

The old man sobered up quickly, and looked at her solemnly. "No."

"Why?"

Bakinu shook his head. "At first exile seems like fun. You're living on your own, being independent, doing what you want. But after a while the loneliness gets to you."

"But I won't be lonely," Cara insisted. "I'll have you."

"It doesn't matter," Bakinu stated. "You'll never be able to see your friends or family again. It's harder than you think, living on your own. There's no one to depend on, and no one to help you. Most people can't bear it."

Cara stuck her chin up defiantly. "I can do it. I'm tired of being forced to learn about the Creator, and I don't want to go back."

"No."

"You sound like my father."

"Cara," the old man said, shaking his head again. "I made the same mistake you're making right now. I chose exile over hiding my beliefs, and I regret it every day. I won't let you make the same mistake."

Cara sat quietly, mulling over his words.

"I may be free to believe what I want on this hill, but beliefs have consequences. I suffer for my beliefs every day."

Cara looked up at him hopefully. "Then you can come back to the village with me! Just tell them you've changed your mind, and you believe in the Creator now."

"I can't," Bakinu said sadly. "Exile is for life. I can never be accepted in the village again."

Cara sat in sullen silence, unwilling to admit defeat.

Bakinu sighed. "I can see you need some time to think it over. It's high time you go to bed, anyhow." He rose slowly, joints cracking as he stretched to his full height. He crossed to a small cabinet built into the wall and withdrew a spare set of blankets and pillows. "Here," he said, laying them out in front of the fire. "This should keep you warm tonight. Is there anything else you need?"

Cara shook her head.

"Good," the old man said briskly. "We'll talk again in the morning." He walked around the chair and climbed into his bed, pulling the thick blankets up to his chin. The queechee snorted a small puff of flame and then scrambled up after him, curling up near the foot of the bed.

Cara sighed and lay down on the thick blanket, pulling the other one over her body. The fabric was coarse but warm, unlike any she had felt before. She closed her eyes, and before she knew it she fell into a deep sleep.

A strong tangy smell floated across the small cottage to Cara. She woke with a start, and blinked at the bright sunlight pouring through the window. The fire had gone out and only cold black lumps lay in the fireplace.

"One more," said a voice from the kitchen. A loud snort erupted, followed by a bright burst of flame that lasted for several seconds. "Good girl," Bakinu murmured. The old man emerged from the kitchen carrying two plates, with the queechee perched on one shoulder. A thin trail of smoke drifted from one nostril.

Cara shrugged off the blanket and sat up, blinking groggily. By the brightness of the sun, she judged it to be closer to noon than sunrise.

"Good, you're finally awake," said the old man, setting one plate before her. "Ah, to be young again. I haven't been able to sleep that deeply for years."

Cara looked down at her plate curiously, ignoring his remarks. There was a strange sort of substance, white on the outside and yellow in the middle, with slightly charred parts all around. The yellow part was more liquid than solid, and there were some small purple flecks sprinkled on top.

"What is this?" Cara asked tentatively, poking at it with the fork from her plate.

"Belknay eggs," Bakinu replied. "With sliced up Junga fruit mixed in."

Cara's eyes widened. "Eggs? From belknay? But that's against the law!"

Bakinu chuckled, walking back over to his large armchair and sinking into it with his plate on his lap. "Animals and their byproducts may be considered holy in the village, but I have no such misconceptions here."

Cara smiled. "Oh, right. I never thought about it that way."

"The blankets are also made of odenpom hair."

Cara's eyes got even wider. "Odenpom hair? You must be mad!"

Bakinu smiled. "It was a little dangerous. My odenpom never liked queechees, and Cheea wasn't very fond of her either."

Cara laughed. "No wonder the blanket was so coarse. What happened to it?"

A sad look appeared in the old man's eyes. "Several years ago, a group of rowdy villagers attacked my cottage. They burned down part of the kitchen and stole my odenpom. They claimed

I didn't have the right to own any of the Creator's gifts. Luckily they couldn't catch the belknay."

"Oh…I'm sorry." Cara turned her attention back to the plate in front of her. She took a slow bite, and was shocked by the wild variety of flavors bursting across her tongue. She smiled and then quickly finished the rest, trying in vain to savor each bite. The queechee sat in front of the old man, staring at him expectantly. Bakinu ignored her, focusing on his plate, until she chirped and snorted a small finger of flame at his knee. Bakinu started in his chair, almost dropping his plate, and checked his knee to make sure the flames hadn't damaged his trousers. Grumbling, he reached into his pocket and tossed a small belknay egg at the queechee. She extended her neck and caught it gently between her sharp teeth. To Cara's surprise, the queechee swallowed the egg whole, the huge lump showing clearly as it slid down the queechee's thin neck.

"How did you train her to cook food?" Cara asked, setting down her plate and looking at the queechee curiously.

Bakinu chuckled. "Cheea? Even if I wanted to, I can't control her. Frying the food was her idea. I think that's how they prefer to eat in the wild. She found me almost ten years ago, and I haven't had to cook my own food since then."

"It's a shame they're so dangerous. Even the church won't protect them."

Bakinu smiled. "Imagine if they were bigger."

Cara repressed a laugh. "They'd be unstoppable! The entire valley would be in flames."

"Giant queechees are supposed to live in the mountains."

Cara involuntarily looked north, trying to see the distant towering peaks.

"They breathe ice instead of fire, and they grow larger than trees."

Cara snorted. "Okay, now you're just making things up."

The old man smiled. "How about an invisible intangible giant queechee?"

"A what?"

"A queechee that cannot be seen and cannot be felt. I have one in my kitchen."

Cara laughed. "No you don't!"

The old man raised one eyebrow. "Prove it."

Cara smirked. "Just look! There's no queechee there. And how would it fit?"

The old man smiled. "Ah, but didn't I say it was invisible? You can't see it. And it's intangible, so it can walk right through walls. It can easily fit in that kitchen."

Cara frowned. "Well then I'd hear it. Something that large is bound to make some sort of noise."

"Good thinking. But I forgot to mention that it's also inaudible. It doesn't make any sounds."

Cara shook her head. "Now that's just stupid. How can I prove that it's not there if you can't see, hear, or touch it?"

Bakinu shrugged. "You can't prove it. You just have to take my word for it. The giant queechee could be there right now."

Cara cocked her head. "No it's not! It doesn't make sense. You should have to prove that it's there, not the other way around."

Bakinu smiled. "Exactly. There's no way to prove the queechee is there, but there's no way to prove that the queechee isn't there. You just have to take it on faith."

Cara grinned as his point suddenly became clear. "Oh, I see. The queechee is like the Creator."

Bakinu laughed again. "Very good! You're very quick, Cara. Most believers ask you to disprove their faith with facts, but for everything else in life we ask for the burden of proof to be with the believer. Why should things be any different with religion?"

Cara fiddled with her empty plate on the floor. "I don't know where we came from or how people were created, but everyone says the Creator did it. How can they all be wrong?"

Bakinu slowly chewed the last of his eggs and fruit, pondering her question. "It's hard to question established beliefs. A long time ago someone probably asked that very same question – where do we all come from? And rather than try and find out, it was attributed to religion. An omnipotent omniscient being that created everything in existence. The Creator."

Cara frowned again. "Omni…what?"

"Omnipotent. It means unlimited power. And omniscience means knowing everything."

"How do you know all of these words?"

Bakinu gave a wry smile. "Believe it or not, I used to be a priest."

Cara gasped. "You! A priest?"

Bakinu shrugged. "It's not so hard to believe. I was curious about the world. I wanted to know how it worked and where things came from. And since the Creator is responsible for these things, I thought the best way to learn would be to study the Creator."

"What made you become an atheist?"

"I found that the Penlet didn't actually answer any of my questions. It spends most of its time praising the Creator for his deeds instead of explaining how he accomplished them. And things just didn't add up. He is supposed to know about everything we do, and he is supposed to be able to do anything at any time. A rather unbelievable concept, if you ask me. Just because we don't know how something works doesn't mean that the Creator made it."

Cara's eyes flew open. "That's what I said yesterday that got me into trouble! I asked why the Creator would let bad things happen in the world if he knows that they're going to happen and he can stop it. And then my teacher gave me a reprimand token." She looked down at her plate, suddenly reminded of home. Her father must be worried sick about her by now. To her surprise she felt a little guilty. He did mean well, even if he was wrong.

Bakinu looked at her carefully. "You need to go back, you know. You still have a family that cares about you, even if you do have disagreements."

"But I don't believe anymore," Cara burst out. "How can I? Everything makes so much more sense when you describe it. My father will never let me be an atheist. I can't go home."

Bakinu set his plate on the table and leaned forward earnestly. "Cara, you know you can't stay. Your father is surely looking for you by now, and sooner or later he will find you here. You belong at home with your family."

Cara shook her head stubbornly. "No, I don't. He doesn't care about me."

Bakinu sighed, then slowly stood up, picking up Cara's plate and his own. "He does, even if it doesn't feel like it now. He just worries what will happen to you as an atheist. And he has good reason to – just look at me." The old man smiled sadly then walked to the kitchen and set the plates down.

"But how am I supposed to live with him?" Cara called out, a little desperate at the thought of returning home to her father.

Bakinu walked back into the room and held out a scrap of meat for Cheea. She leapt from the rug in front of the fireplace and zoomed on outstretched wings across the room, snatching the meat from Bakinu's hand with surprising agility. She landed on the back of the armchair and worried at the meat, ripping it in half with her sharp teeth.

"You'll have to lie," Bakinu said absently, watching Cheea savage the meat scraps.

"Lie?"

"Yes," Bakinu said, his voice gaining strength. "It's the only way. You'll have to pretend to believe in the Creator. You can enjoy the benefit of friends and family without living in ignorance. And maybe, someday, you'll be able to tell the truth to someone. Someone else who doubts the Creator."

"Maybe," Cara said doubtfully.

Bakinu's eyes had a fervent glow to them. "When you have kids someday you can raise them as atheists, and the truth will spread. One day your children's children might be able to live in a world without the Creator. Imagine that. A world without religion!"

Cara frowned. "When I have kids? Hang on, I never said…"

BANG BANG BANG The front door shuddered as a fist pounded on its surface.

"Open up! In the name of the High Priest, open this door, you filthy baki!"

Chapter Five

Bakinu froze, staring at the door. The blood drained from his face as his eyes grew wide with fear. Cara looked at Bakinu in surprise.

BANG BANG BANG

"Open up I say! Or we'll break this door down!"

Bakinu started at the noise, then rushed to the door and opened it quickly. Bright sunlight spilled through the doorway, framing two tall men dressed in flowing robes. Serious expressions lined their faces as they looked down at Bakinu's slight frame.

"Careful with the door, please," Bakinu said meekly. "It took me weeks to make a new one after you broke it down last time."

The taller priest looked at him disdainfully. "Then maybe we should break it down again."

The other priest interrupted, shooting the taller priest a warning glance. "We're looking for a young girl, thirteen years old with golden brown hair. Have you seen her?"

Before Bakinu could respond, the taller priest noticed Cara, still sitting on the odenpom blanket in the middle of the room. His eyes grew wide and he strode forward, grabbing Bakinu by the collar and thrusting him against a wall. "How dare you lay a hand on the High Priest's daughter! If you have harmed her in any way…"

"No!" Cara yelled, leaping to her feet. "Leave him alone! He was helping me!"

A flash of wings dashed across the room, accompanied by an ear-splitting battle screech. A flash of claws and sharp teeth hit the priest with a whirl, and a splash of blood squirted onto the door and ceiling.

"AAAARGGHHH!" the priest yelled, letting go of Bakinu and jumping away, clutching his bloody arm in agony. Bakinu staggered back into the room and fell on the floor. The other priest drew a knife and thrust it at the flying queechee. Cheea dodged, spinning away in midair before landing on the ground between the priests and Bakinu. She opened her mouth and shot a large burst of flame in the direction of the priests. They leapt back as the fire singed their toes.

"STOP!" screamed Cara, jumping to her feet. Everyone grew very still as they glared at each other from across the room.

"That animal needs to be killed," the injured priest growled, still nursing his arm.

"Never," growled Bakinu.

"I said stop!" repeated Cara loudly. "Bakinu helped me last night. He gave me food and shelter when I was lost in these hills, and he was going to help me get home today. You have no reason to punish him or his queechee."

The priest frowned. "It attacked me!"

"After you attacked Bakinu," scolded Cara, whirling to face the injured priest. "If you touch them again, I'll tell my father what you did."

47

The priests gave her a wary look.

Cara glared back at them, eyes narrowed. "Give me a minute to say goodbye, then we can go back to the village." After waiting for a reluctant nod from the priests, she quickly turned and went to Bakinu. She extended her hand and helped him to his feet. "Are you okay?" she asked quietly.

Bakinu brushed himself off, shaking a little. "Yes, I'm fine now. Thank you for stepping in." He smiled shakily, his watery blue eyes tearing up slightly. "I guess this is goodbye."

Cara leaned forward and hugged him tightly. He stiffened for a second, unaccustomed to affection, then relaxed slightly and hugged her back. One of the priests grunted his disapproval from the doorway.

"I'll miss you," Cara whispered before letting go. She broke off the hug and then turned around, walking through the front door and joining the priests as they left the house.

"Goodbye!" she called out, waving to Bakinu. He stood at the doorway and waved back. Cheea fluttered to his shoulder and trilled, blood still shining on her claws. Cara turned and followed the priests as they strode south through the long green grasses. Within minutes they crested the hill and Bakinu and the cottage fell out of sight.

It was a beautiful day. The sun pulsed high in the sky, almost directly overhead. A light breeze swept over the grasses, creating a melody of rustling stalks and sighing stems. The hills provided Cara with a spectacular view of the valley. Orderly rows of crops created geometrical patterns around the farms of her village, nestled between the rolling hills of the land. She could even make out the tiny cluster of buildings around the village center.

"It's a wonderful day for a walk, isn't it?" she said cheerfully. One of the priests grunted in approval, but avoided making eye contact with her. Cara turned her attention to her escorts. She recognized them. John and Paul, if she remembered correctly. John still cradled his bloody arm close to his body. Long shallow gashes ran from his elbow to his wrist. They walked stiffly on either side of her, eyes looking everywhere but at her. She could tell that her friendship with Bakinu disturbed them deeply. She smiled at the thought. They must be so infuriated that she was the High Priest's daughter – they couldn't say anything to her.

"How long did it take you to find me?" she asked.

John, the taller priest, looked at her reluctantly. "We've been searching the hills ever since you disappeared," he said gruffly. "Your father is very worried about you. He'll be glad to see that you're safe."

Another pang of guilt hit Cara. How many priests were out searching for her right now? Knowing her father, he probably sent the entire church out looking for her. She was certainly in for a big lecture when she got home.

The group walked in silence for a few hours, trekking slowly downwards as they descended into the valley. The gnarled Junga trees that dotted the hills began to disappear, and the breeze that chilled the tops of the hills seemed unable to reach them. Several flocks of iraa birds flew overhead, throwing small torrents of rain to the valley beneath them. Cara had trouble focusing on the scenery around her. All she could think about was the upcoming conversation with her father. What was he going to do to her? What was she going to say to him? She was used to lying to him about small things, but would he believe her if she lied to him about the Creator?

It was well in the afternoon when they finally made it back to the church. Cara's stomach churned with hunger and her legs were quite tired after the long walk, but she wasn't allowed to rest. John and Paul marched her straight to her father's office, knocking lightly on the heavy oak door. Cara stared at its intricate carvings with apprehension.

"Come," said a tired voice from inside. The priests opened the door and ushered Cara through.

Her father sat at his desk in the richly decorated room, lines of fatigue etched across his face. He looked up slowly, ready for more disappointing news, and froze at the sight of Cara. For a moment he just stared, unable to speak, then he leapt from his desk and rushed towards her with surprising agility. Cara blinked in surprise as he embraced her tightly, a gesture very uncharacteristic for him. *Does this mean I'm not in trouble?*

"You're okay," her father whispered, squeezing gently. He slowly released her, stepping back and holding her in front of him by her shoulders. "Where have you been, Cara? I've been worried sick…" He trailed off and looked at the priests.

Paul cleared his throat. "We found her at the heretic's house. Bakinu gave her shelter and food overnight. We brought her straight here."

The High Priest frowned. "Bakinu?" He looked at Cara warily. "We have a lot to talk about, I see. Thank you, Paul; thank you, John. You may call off the search now. Please spread the word to the rest of the priests."

John and Paul nodded their heads respectfully, then stepped out of the room, closing the heavy door gently behind them.

The High Priest gazed at Cara, his expression slowly shifting from worry to irritation. "Bakinu, Cara? How did you find that blasphemer?"

Cara frowned. "It's not like I did it on purpose. I was tired and cold and hungry, and I saw the light on in his cottage. And he's not..." she trailed off, remembering Bakinu's advice. She had to pretend to believe in the Creator, and that meant she couldn't defend his disbelief.

"What were you thinking, running away like that? You could have ended up anywhere! When I saw that you had jumped on a scutney..." he trailed off and gazed at her softly, stroking her hair with his right hand. "I could have lost you forever, Cara. You realize that, don't you?"

Cara fought the urge to step back. She was unnerved by her father's uncharacteristic show of affection, but she didn't want him to start yelling at her either. Instead, she bowed her head and looked at the floor, as if she were ashamed. *I'm glad I ran away,* she secretly thought. *Otherwise I never would have met Bakinu.*

The High Priest sighed, then slowly turned and walked back to his desk. He sat down slowly and gazed at Cara carefully. She stared back apprehensively, wondering what was coming next.

"Cara," he began slowly, "as glad as I am to see you back safely, I cannot ignore your actions or the words you said before."

Cara's heart dropped like a rock. Here it was. The other shoe.

"Your disrespect for the Creator and your willingness to disobey me must be rectified. Your future in this community rests on this fact. I will have to think deeply on this matter, and I will have to ask the Creator for guidance."

This is it, I have to start lying now. "I know I was wrong, father," Cara interrupted. "I was wrong to insult the Creator. I do believe in Him, and I know that He has given us everything."

The High Priest eyed her warily. "Even if that is so, I cannot ignore your actions. I want you to go to your room for the rest of the day and read the Penlet. Maybe you will find some of the answers to your questions in its holy pages. I will have food and water sent to your room. Do you understand my instructions?"

Cara nodded, hardly able to believe her ears.

"Good. Now go." He gazed at her seriously. "And don't go near that heretic Bakinu again."

Cara fought hard to keep her face neutral, nodding quickly before spinning around and exiting the room. She closed the door behind her, making sure it latched, and then burst into a silent peal of giggles. *My room? He sent me to my room?* The last time she had been sent to her room was when she had stolen a batch of cookies from the church kitchens when she was eight. This wasn't a punishment; it was a slap on the wrist!

An apprentice priest across the room looked up from his job of straightening Penlets in the pews and stared at her disapprovingly. Cara forced the smile off her face and tried to look grim as she slowly shuffled off towards the back of the church. She walked down several small corridors behind the main chamber and then slipped into her room, a small, cozy chamber with a thick carpet and brightly colored walls. She closed the door behind her, dashed to her bed, and leapt onto the embroidered quilt covering its surface. She bounced onto her back, smiling widely, and lay there for a few minutes, hands behind her head as she stared at the ceiling.

"What good luck," she said aloud, listening to her voice bounce around the room. She grinned. Everything was perfect. Who would ever guess that running away from home would make life so much easier. She gazed around the room. Several small tapestries featuring small cavorting animals hung from the walls. Her mother had woven them long ago, shortly after Cara was born. Her mother had died years ago, but she had always been the opposite of her father – caring, loving, and understanding. The utilitarian bookshelf across the room was a gift from her father. It was painted with scenes from the Penlet – a constant reminder to his daughter of her connection to the Creator. It was so typical of her father. Duty always came before family.

Tap tap tap A gentle knock sounded on the door.

"Yes?" Cara called, propping herself up on the bed.

An apprentice priest slowly opened the door, balancing a small tray of food in one hand. "The High Priest asked me to bring you this," he stuttered, avoiding eye contact with Cara.

Cara grinned at his awkwardness. "Put it down on the table there. You may go now."

The young man didn't move. "And I'm...I'm...I'm supposed to make sure you're reading the Penlet." His eyes nervously flicked up to hers and then over at the Penlet sitting on the bookshelf.

Cara raised her eyebrow, ready to give the boy an earful, but then she remembered Bakinu's words. She sighed, slowly stood up, and picked up the Penlet from the bookshelf, returning to her bed and opening up to a random page. "There, I'm reading now. Are you happy?"

The apprentice priest nodded hurriedly and rushed out of the room, closing the door quickly behind him.

I might as well play the role of dutiful daughter, she thought wearily. She stared at the page and started reading.

"And Chalazion stood up and spake to the crowd, saying, 'Be warned, good people, for the end of days is yet to come. Remember these caves, and remember these words. In a period of peace and prosperity there will be a loss of faith and a loss of lives. Bright bolts of light will arc down from the heavens under clear skies, and the Creator's gifts will be slaughtered in great numbers. An unearthly roar will echo through the heart of the land, and the people will know unbounded fear. The Dursturock will return.'"

"Hah," Cara burst out aloud. "Dursturock my foot. I bet they made up the whole story for this dumb book." She smiled. It felt good to voice her doubts out loud. She flipped to an earlier section and read some more.

"The Creator, in his wisdom, took pity on the people. With Chalazion as his tool he brought them safety and security in their time of greatest need. The

prophet Chalazion spoke with His voice and listened with His patience. And when the Dursturock had passed, the people knew His words to be the words of the Creator. For the prophet is one with the Creator, and will come again to defeat the Dursturock and save the land from its wrath."

Cara snorted out loud. She reached for the table and grabbed the tray of food the apprentice priest left there while thumbing through the pages, looking for a more interesting section to read. She slowly spooned the grain mash into her mouth and grimaced as it touched her tongue. The mash was bland, as always. *Nowhere near as good as Bakinu's eggs and fruit,* she found herself thinking. She suddenly had a pang of regret. He must be so lonely now, in his little cottage way up in the hills. *Maybe I should have stayed up there...*

A bookmark slid out of the pages as Cara thumbed through them. She caught it quickly, before it fell out completely. She carefully opened to the bookmarked page, and frowned at the sight. The Commandments sprawled across the page, an unpleasant reminder of the tedious memorizing Cara had to do as a young girl. She could still remember her father's stern voice, telling her she wasn't to go out and play until she had another Commandment memorized. She slammed the book shut, angry at the memory. Frustrated and bored, she stared at the ceiling for a while. The fatigue from the long walk started to overcome her, and she napped.

Several hours later a gentle tapping echoed through the room. Cara opened her eyes, suddenly awake, and blinked quickly, trying to get her bearings. The sun must have set while she was napping – the room was completely dark. She shivered suddenly. Without a fire in the room, the air had gotten quite cold.

Tap tap tap

"Come in," she said groggily, her voice cracking slightly. She clumsily rubbed the sleep from her eyes as the door opened slowly.

Another apprentice priest stood at the door, but this one was slightly taller and thinner. He bowed respectfully, nodding his head to his chest. He brushed black hair out of his dark eyes and squinted through the darkness, balancing a small tray of food in one hand. "Would you like me to light a fire, Chandra?"

Cara frowned, slowly sitting up in her bed. "Um, yeah, I guess. You can leave the food on the table."

The apprentice priest carefully placed the tray on the table, then slowly lit the kindling in the fireplace with a candle from a sconce in the hallway. Once the flames were strong, he returned to the doorway and waited, eyes carefully leveled at the bookshelf on the far wall.

Cara eyed him wearily. No doubt this boy would tell her father that she had not been reading the Penlet. And that's the last thing she needed right now.

"I was reading, you know," she said defensively, reaching for the plate of food. "I had only just put down my Penlet to take a nap when you knocked. See? It's right here on my bed."

The apprentice priest turned his dark brown eyes towards hers. "I believe you."

Cara frowned. "You do?"

The apprentice priest smiled. "Of course. And even if you lied, I'm sure you have a very good reason to. So I believe you."

Cara blinked, taken aback by his honesty. "Okay. Thanks I guess. You may go now."

The apprentice priest didn't move.

Cara cleared her throat. "I said you may leave now," she repeated a little louder. What was the matter with this guy?

The apprentice priest bowed his head. "I'm sorry Chandra, but I can't do that. Your father has instructed me to watch over you. I am not to leave your side until he deems otherwise."

Chapter Six

"You're what?" Cara said, her jaw dropping open. *Is he serious?*

"Your father would like you perform your animal chores this evening, and he wishes me to accompany you. Are you ready to do them now, or would you like to eat first?"

Cara examined him carefully. She had seen him around the church before, but he was just another apprentice priest – a mindless slave to her father. Now that she looked at him closely, she could see that his face was young – almost as young as hers.

"How old are you?" she asked accusingly.

"Fifteen," he answered calmly.

She frowned. "Then you shouldn't be wearing those robes. Apprentice priests have to be at least 16 years old."

He looked down at his robes, fingering the flowing red cloth with care. "Your father made an exception in my case. I was allowed to leave school last year to begin my duties as an apprentice priest."

She frowned. "I don't remember you from school."

The apprentice priest smiled. "I remember you."

"What's your name then?" she asked accusingly.

"Leolin."

Cara raised her eyebrows. "Leolin? I thought you were still in school. You're that quiet kid who's always reading."

Leolin smiled again. "Yes, that was me."

Cara gazed at him carefully. "You look different in those robes. Why would you want to become a priest, of all things?"

Leolin looked fondly at the Penlet on Cara's bed. "The same reason as everyone else. I wish to serve the Creator, and show Him my gratitude. I am truly blessed in that I've been permitted to serve Him at my age."

Cara fought hard to keep the sneer of disgust from her face. There was no need to give Leolin any reason to doubt her beliefs. Not if he was working for her father.

"So if you're such a valuable servant, then why are you wasting your time with me?"

"You are not a waste of time, Chandra," Leolin said earnestly. "None of us are, you of all people should know that. We are all the Creator's children."

"I don't see you babysitting anyone else," shot back Cara.

Leolin nodded solemnly. "It is true. You are the High Priest's daughter. And as his daughter, you deserve special care. Your father is worried about you, and he asked me to help you find your way back to the Creator."

Cara stiffened. "He told you?"

Leolin gazed at her sorrowfully. "He told me that you were angry and spoke out against the Creator. He worries about your faith, and he knows this matter must be handled carefully. I am here to help you Chandra, not to judge you."

Cara choked down her angry retort. She struggled in silence for a few moments, before deciding it was better not to respond at all. She quickly jumped to her feet and strode to her wardrobe, throwing on a warm cloak before brushing past Leolin on her way to do her chores.

Help me? she thought furiously. *I'll make his life a living hell. No one babysits me.* Leolin's light footsteps followed her as she rushed through the hallways and into the barn. The room was dark – the moonlight had trouble penetrating the small windows and thickly thatched roof. Cara grabbed a lantern from the hallway and swung it around, throwing flickering fingers of light onto the walls of the barn. Heavy metal tools hung neatly from pegs on the walls, and large sacks of feed lay in a pile in a corner of the barn. She grabbed a bag of feed and stomped into the yard, with Leolin trailing behind her.

A full moon shined brightly overhead, casting a soft light over the animals in the yard. Cara performed her chores silently and furiously, quickly filling the troughs in the area with grain and fresh water. Two odenpom turned into boulders as she stormed by them in the yard, and one belknay began to flash in alarm when she nearly kicked it. Leolin watched in silence, following her like a shadow as she stomped from place to place. She finally slowed down when she was laying fresh straw on the dirt floor of the barn. She glanced at Leolin out of the corner of her eye. He had a content expression on his face as he looked around at the barn, gazing over some of the odenpom that had wandered into the barn. *How can he be so happy?* she thought resentfully. Any other priest would have been angry at having to follow her around everywhere. Her attitude and rebelliousness were no secret in the village, and she did nothing to hide her contempt for the priests.

"This is a waste of your time, you know," she said suddenly, breaking the silence.

Leolin shifted his gaze from the odenpom to Cara's face. "What is?"

Cara waved her hand over the barn. "This. Watching me. I'm just doing chores. I've never had a problem doing them before, so why should you waste your valuable time watching me do them? Don't you have better things to do?"

Leolin shrugged. "I live to serve the Creator. If He has deemed that it is important for me to watch you do chores, then that is what I must do."

Cara frowned. How could he be so passive? She grabbed a shovel and swept up a pile of odenpom dung, throwing it into a bucket in the corner of the room. "What would you be doing right now, if you didn't have to be here?" she carefully asked, trying to sound nonchalant.

"I would be preparing for my confirmation," Leolin said wistfully, staring out the window.

"Your confirmation?" Cara asked incredulously. "You're only fifteen. You can't become a confirmed priest until you're at least eighteen!"

Leolin shrugged. "Nevertheless, it is what I want to do. Preparing for confirmation is a lifelong process. There are many tasks I must perform to prove myself worthy of the honor."

Cara smirked. "Well then Leolin, you should take the night off. Go ahead and work on your tasks. I'll be fine here; you don't need to watch me anymore."

Leolin bowed his head. "Your concern for my happiness is touching, but I cannot do as you say. I made a promise to your father that I would watch over you, and nothing can come before that promise."

Cara scowled, losing her patience. "I don't need you, okay? This is a waste of your time and mine. You've only been assigned to watch me because you're the only one stupid enough to actually do it. Any other priest would have taken my father's orders a little less literally and only would have checked up on me from time to time."

Leolin blinked, a little surprised by her sudden hostility. "I'm sorry you feel that way, Chandra…"

"It's Cara, you dolt. Cara!"

"…Cara," Leolin said carefully, "…but your father's instructions were clear. I cannot leave you alone."

Cara glared at him, fuming. "Fine," she shot back. "You can at least help me with my chores then." Cara grabbed another shovel off the wall and tossed it at Leolin. The shovel flew through the air directly at his chest, and he barely caught the long wooden handle before it smacked him in the face. The heavy metal tip caught on his neat red robes and smeared dung across the cloth. Cara smirked at the sight.

Leolin took a deep breath and smiled, averting his eyes from his soiled robes. "Of course, Chan…Cara. If you wish." He leaned over and scooped up another pile of odenpom dung. Cara smiled triumphantly at the sight.

The rest of the chores were completed rather quickly. Cara hated to admit it, but Leolin was a hard and efficient worker. He completed nearly twice the amount of work that she did in the same amount of time, and he did it all with a smile on his face. His patience only made Cara more furious. When they finally finished, Cara hung the shovels on their pegs and returned to the church, striding through the well-lit corridors towards her chamber. When she reached her chamber door, she paused and glared at Leolin.

"You're *not* following me in here. I don't care what my father said."

Leolin bowed his head. "I bid you good night, Cara." He slowly turned and walked back down the corridor in the direction of the priests' quarters.

Cara sighed in relief and entered her room. She took of her soiled clothes and placed them in the laundry basket. One of the perks of being the High Priest's daughter was that she didn't have to do her own laundry – the apprentice priests washed the clothes of everyone living in the church. She bathed quickly in the washroom adjoining her chambers, and then slipped into a nightdress. The small fire in the fireplace threw flickering shadows on the dark walls of the room, warming her bare feet as she walked across the floor to her bed. She climbed slowly under the covers, and was asleep in no time at all.

A loud clamor of bells woke Cara the next morning. A few beams of early morning sunlight trickled through the windows on the eastern wall, illuminating the smooth wooden floors and the brightly colored tapestries. Cara yawned, standing up and running her hand through her hair. She walked to the wash-room and splashed some water on her face. For once she felt well rested. The nap during her time out yesterday had really refreshed her.

Cara pulled on a new set of clothes and opened her door. Leolin stood in the middle of the hallway, an annoyingly cheerful smile plastered across his young face. Cara noticed he was dressed in freshly laundered red robes.

"Really?" she said, her heart sinking. "I haven't even had time to eat yet!"

Leolin held out a piece of fruit. "We'd better hurry. You don't have much time to finish your chores before you need to leave for school."

Cara rolled her eyes and brushed past him, snatching the fruit from his hands. She grabbed a brush from the barn and headed into the yard, quickly weaving her way through the odenpom and belknay. The dirt in the yard was slightly squishy under her shoes. It must have rained last night – she could see drops of water still glistening on the patches of grass in the yard. She found her three odenpom near the side of the barn, grazing contentedly on the long grass there. She approached them carefully, talking soothingly to let them know it was her. She knelt next to the one by the barn door and slowly began to groom it, struggling to pull the comb through its shaggy brown coat.

She glanced over at Leolin. To her surprise, he had also grabbed a comb from the barn, and he was grooming one of the other odenpom. He was quite good at it. The comb hardly caught at all as he ran it smoothly through the odenpom's coat. Cara snorted in disgust and turned her attention back to the animal in front of her.

With Leolin's help, she finished her chores far faster than she ever had before. Within twenty minutes they had groomed the odenpom, refilled the food and water troughs near the barn, and mucked out the yard near the barn doors. Cara couldn't help but admire Leolin's efficiency. No wonder her father had let him graduate a year early – the boy was a wonder child.

Cara returned to her room and grabbed her Penlet. She turned back to the corridor, where Leolin stood waiting.

"So, uh, thanks for your help, I guess," she said reluctantly, avoiding eye contact with him. "I'll see you after school." She turned and started walking down the corridor, relieved to finally be free of him.

"Wait, Cara," Leolin called out, chasing after her. "I'm coming with you."

Cara whirled around. "You're what?"

Leolin looked at her sympathetically. "I have to keep an eye on you at all times, especially when you're at school. It was part of your father's instructions."

Cara narrowed her eyes. "He would never…"

Leolin shrugged apologetically. "I'm sorry. Those were his orders."

"You can't though. People will ask questions. How will you explain…"

"He already thought of that," interjected Leolin. "No one will know that I'm here to help you recover your beliefs. Instead, I have been given the task of assisting the school teacher as a requirement for my Confirmation test. I will assist Mr. Baynor in teaching the lessons of the Penlet, and I will begin teaching certain advanced students how to write."

Cara laughed derisively. "You? Teach people how to write? You've only been an apprentice priest for a year. How could you possibly know how to write that well?"

"I'm a quick learner," Leolin said earnestly. "I've been writing ever since I became an apprentice priest. Your father thinks that I can teach some of the basic principles to the most promising students."

Cara snorted in anger and whirled away, stomping out of the church and down the road towards the village center. Her long angry strides put her far ahead of Leolin, and he had to jog to keep up. After ten minutes or so she finally slowed down, her legs aching slightly from the fast pace. Leolin caught up and finally walked alongside her, panting ever so slightly. Tall crops on either side of the road waved in a light breeze as the sun continued to rise over the valley. Rain drops glistened on the long stalks as beams of light reflected off of their sides. Small puddles of rainwater collected at the sides of the dirt road, but the slightly elevated center stayed high and dry. Cara scuffed the ground with her toe and glanced sideways at Leolin.

"Why do you believe in the Creator?" she blurted out.

Leolin looked at her in surprise. "Why wouldn't I?"

"You're smart, you're talented. You're literally the best in the class. So why do you believe in Him?"

Leolin smiled sadly. "I think the more reasonable question is why don't you believe in Him?"

Cara frowned. "Don't turn this back on me. Your job is to help me believe again, so start talking. Why should I believe in the Creator?"

Leolin blinked in surprise. "Why, because he is the Creator. He exists. He created us, this world, the animals…everything. Without Him we are nothing. He revealed Himself to us to help us live our lives in peace, and His wisdom is what guides our lives to the path of righteousness."

"Where's your proof?"

"The Penlet says it is so."

Cara snorted. "That's all?"

Leolin looked at her sadly. "I also feel His presence in my heart and in my soul. The Creator is love, and He is all around us."

"I don't feel his presence."

"You just need to open yourself to His glory. It is then that you will know true happiness."

Cara cocked an eyebrow. "I'm happy not believing in Him. Why does He need my belief so badly?"

Leolin looked at her, his eyes earnest and unblinking. "Are you happy Cara?"

Cara flushed a deep red and stared at the well-worn path in the center of the road, averting her eyes from Leolin's gaze. As much as she didn't want to admit it, he had a point. She did not feel happy. Not now, and not for a long time. Not like that smug satisfied dopey grin that Leolin always seemed to have. But would believing in a pretend being that did all the thinking for her really make her happy? She shook her head, frustrated, shoving her hands into her pockets.

"He doesn't need your faith," Leolin continued softly. "He simply wants what is best for us. By believing in Him we will follow a path of virtue and justice…"

Cara kicked a stone angrily. "I'm living a moral life just fine without His guidance."

"That's because you are surrounded by those who believe," Leolin said confidently. "We are a positive influence on you, and we will help you come back to the Creator and His love."

"So what will happen if I don't ever start believing? What will the Creator do to me?"

Leolin looked at her sharply, a worried expression on his face. "If you don't believe in the Creator, then you cannot be accepted into his Kingdom after death. Your spirit will be forever lost, condemned to hell for eternity."

"Even if I lead a moral life? Even if I do more good than most believers do in their lifetimes?" Cara gazed into Leolin's eyes, searching for some sort of opening in his earnest expression. "Come on, Leolin, even that must sound wrong to you."

Leolin shrugged. "It is written in the Penlet. You must believe, or pay the price."

Cara sighed in exasperation and looked to the sky. Large white clouds sailed across a dark blue sky, some trailing wisps of white that looked like little dunbees.

"How about the Commandments then?" she asked suddenly, struck by an idea.

"What about them?"

Cara gazed at Leolin attentively. "If the Creator doesn't need our faith, then why is it such an important part of the Penlet? Just read the Commandments. The first two Commandments explicitly say that we are not allowed to believe in any other faiths, and that if we don't believe in Him then we will be punished. Then the second two go on about honoring and appreciating Him. It isn't until the sixth Commandment that He tells us not to murder!"

Leolin cleared his throat before carefully answering. "Faith in the Creator is important above all else. It is this faith that brings us to the rest of his Commandments."

"You've got to be kidding me." Cara raised her Penlet in front of Leolin, shaking it back and forth. "It's a scam, Leolin! Believe in me or go to hell. And we've all fallen for it."

"The Creator is not a scam, Cara. He is love."

Cara stomped her foot, losing her temper and forgetting Bakinu's words of warning. "If the Creator is love, then why is there so much pain and suffering in this world? Why is there murder, when the Creator is all powerful? Either the Creator is evil, unjust, and indifferent, or He doesn't exist. And given the lack of proof that He exists at all, I find it easier to believe the latter."

Leolin studied her carefully, a frown etched across his young face. "We have more work to do than I realized." And he touched his fingers to his forehead and started a silent prayer.

Chapter Seven

Cara bit down on her tongue angrily. It was like talking to an odenpom! *This isn't helping anything.* The more she argued the more she would have to lie in the long run. Bakinu was right. Lying was the only way she would be able to live in peace. She glared reluctantly at Leolin. His brow was furrowed as he looked at the ground, mumbling to himself in prayer. She could tell he was disturbed by her beliefs, but he was too honorable to yell at her because of them.

"Why are you helping me, anyway?" she asked, curious.

Leolin sighed, stopping his prayers. "Because your father…"

"No, no, not that," Cara interrupted. "He could have ordered a lot of priests to fix my beliefs, but most of them would be more comfortable exiling me than fixing me. So why are you so willing to help?"

Leolin pushed a lock of black hair out of his eyes, staring up at the sky. "I believe that everyone is worth saving. Unlike some of my colleagues, I believe that all souls, no matter how far they stray, deserved to be saved. The Penlet teaches us that forgiveness is a lesson we must never forget, and I have taken the Creator's lesson to heart." He turned his gaze from the sky and stared at Cara solemnly. "Know that I am here for you, Cara. I will help you find your way back to the Creator."

It took all of Cara's strength not to roll her eyes and laugh at his sincerity. She avoided his gaze and looked ahead down the long dirt path. To her astonishment, the weathered wooden walls of the old schoolhouse were already visible through the swaying crops. The sun had finally finished its journey over the surrounding hills of the valley, and its strong rays cut through the chilly morning air to reflect off of the peeling red paint on the side of the school. Cara sighed at the sight, and reluctantly trudged into the building with Leolin at her side.

Mr. Baynor sat at his desk in the front of the large room, hunched over a Penlet on his desk. He looked up at the sound of the door, and froze at the sight of Leolin and Cara.

"Leolin?" he asked, surprised. "Is that you?"

Leolin grinned. "Hello, Mr. Baynor. Nice to see you again."

A wide smile broke over Mr. Baynor's face. Cara hardly recognized him without his customary frown of disapproval. He stood up quickly and crossed the room, embracing Leolin in a tight hug. "It's been a while, my boy. It's good to see you again. How is the priesthood treating you?"

"Very well. It's been an amazing experience."

Mr. Baynor stood back and beamed at him. "You always were my star pupil. The youngest student to become an apprentice priest!" He shot a look at Cara, the usual frown returning to his face. "You could learn a thing or two from this young man, Cara."

Cara glared back at him resentfully, clenching her teeth to keep in her angry retort.

"So what brings you to my humble school house?" Mr. Baynor asked, looking curiously at Leolin.

"I'm here at the High Priest's command," Leolin informed him. "This is to be another Confirmation trial."

Mr. Baynor smiled. "Fantastic! How long will you stay?"

"Until the High Priest decides I have learned the lessons there are to learn here. I've been instructed to identify and help teach the most promising candidates for priesthood."

"What a wonderful idea!" exclaimed Mr. Baynor, his face flushed with excitement. "How may I help you?"

Cara turned away from the conversation and sulked down the aisle, trying to ignore their prattle. She slipped into her customary seat in the back and placed her Penlet on her desk. To her surprise, she noted she was the only student in the room. *This is certainly a first.*

"…it shouldn't take long; I should be finished by the end of today. I'll inform you of my decisions tomorrow, after I consult with the priests back at the church, and we can create a plan of advanced study for the students who pass."

"I'm curious, what age groups do you plan on teaching?"

"I was thinking thirteen and up."

Mr. Baynor glanced at Cara and raised an eyebrow. "Are you certain? Fourteen and up might be a more realistic age for the skills you're looking for."

Leolin shrugged. "I felt ready for these skills at thirteen. Even if no one passes, it doesn't hurt to give them a chance."

Mr. Baynor shrugged. "If that's what you feel is best, then go for it."

A large group of students entered the room, chatting amicably with each other. They quieted when they saw a guest in the room and they looked at him curiously as they sat down in their seats. Leolin smiled pleasantly at them and then resumed his conversation with Mr. Baynor.

"Psst, Cara!" Peter, another student a few years younger than Cara, turned around in his seat and whispered loudly back at her.

Cara glanced up and frowned at his mousy face. "What?" she asked, irritated.

"Who's the priest?"

Cara sighed. "His name is Leolin. He's just an apprentice priest."

Peter's eyebrows shot up. "Leolin? That's Leolin?" He immediately turned away from Cara and started whispering loudly to his friends. Cara snorted in disgust and slouched lower in her chair. This was going to be a bad day.

Over the next ten minutes the schoolhouse filled up quickly. The classroom was buzzing with whispers. No one could remember when they last had a guest at school, and most people in the village didn't get to see priests on a daily basis like Cara. Finally, after the last student ducked into the room, Mr. Baynor cleared his throat and stepped into the center of the room.

"Good morning, class."

"Good morning, Mr. Baynor," chorused four dozen eager students.

"Could everyone please stand for The Creator's Prayer."

Cara reluctantly joined the class as they made the sign of the Creator. When everyone closed their eyes and recited the

Creator's Prayer, she kept her lips tightly sealed. She smirked at all of the heads bowed in prayer around her, but her smirk faded quickly when she saw Leolin open an eye to check on her. She quickly bowed her head and mumbled along.

The class finished the prayer and sat down in unison. Mr. Baynor opened his eyes slowly and beamed at the class.

"I have a great surprise for you today, class. Leolin has come back to our classroom to help teach the wonders of the Penlet. Most of you should remember him – he was your classmate only a year ago."

Many heads nodded around the classroom. The youngest students, the eight-year-olds, looked at Leolin's red robes with awe.

"Leolin was fourteen when he was initiated as an apprentice priest. He is the youngest student ever to have been accepted. His accomplishments do not end there. In the year since he joined the priesthood, he has already transcribed his first Penlet."

Gasps sounded from around the room as students opened their jaws in shock. Even Cara nearly dropped her Penlet on the floor. *He what?* Leolin blushed.

Mr. Baynor smiled, beaming at Leolin proudly. "As you all know, writing is a skill taught only to those in the priesthood. As an apprentice priest, one of the many tasks you must complete is the faithful reproduction of an entire Penlet, word for word."

"How did you do it so fast?" blurted out one young student. His friend next to him looked mortified and shushed him quickly, but Leolin smiled.

"It's a good question. Most apprentice priests spend almost their entire first year just mastering the basic task of writing. It takes time to learn how to form accurate letters with a quill and ink. Since I'm younger, I learned how to write faster than most others. I had more time to write, and I didn't include any drawings. A Penlet with elaborate illustrations and calligraphy takes many years."

The students stared at him in amazement. Mr. Baynor smiled proudly. "Leolin, would you like to describe what your plan is for today?"

Leolin crossed his arms behind his back and surveyed the classroom with kind eyes. "Today I will be meeting with those students who are thirteen or older. There should be nineteen of you in total. I'll ask you to perform several small tests." He paused and smiled kindly. "Don't worry, there isn't anything wrong if you don't pass. This is just a basic test to see if you have any special talents."

The younger students slouched in disappointment, but the older students shot each other excited looks. Cara gritted her teeth, disgusted at their enthusiasm. Didn't they see what was going on? He was selecting candidates for the priesthood!

"Mr. Baynor will lead today's lesson as usual. If you're in the testing group, I'll take you outside in pairs. Each test should take only about thirty minutes." He glanced at Mr. Baynor. "I'd like to call up the first pair now, if that is possible. Can I start with the youngest group?"

"Of course," Mr. Baynor replied. "We have four thirteen-year-olds. Let's start with George and Chandra."

George, a small skinny kid with unkempt red hair, leapt to his feet and strode to the front of the room, a proud smile on his face. Cara reluctantly stood up and followed him.

"Wonderful," Leolin exclaimed. "Let's get started! Follow me please." He turned and walked out of the classroom, his long red robes swirling around his legs. George followed him eagerly, nearly tripping over his own feet in excitement.

"Behave yourself, Cara," Mr. Baynor said quietly, shooting her a warning glance. Cara glared back angrily before following Leolin out the door.

She stepped onto the dirt road and took a deep breath of the fresh morning air. George was already sitting on one of the benches that lined the large dirt clearing, and Leolin stood nearby, gazing over the swaying crops surrounding the village center. Cara slowly shuffled across the yard and sat down on the bench next to him, scuffing the dirt nearby with her toe.

Leolin turned his attention to the two students on the bench, smiling broadly. "I think we'll start with some basic transcribing exercises." He reached into a fold of his robes and withdrew two large flat plates of a strange sort of rock. "These are writing tablets. Apprentice priests use them to practice forming pictures and letters. Only when a pupil masters the basic letters and shapes are they allowed to use parchment. As you both know, parchment is very hard to make, so it's only used for transcribing Penlets." He stepped forward and handed the tablets to Cara and George.

Cara held the tablet carefully. It was surprisingly thin. The surface of the rock was shiny and smooth to the touch. The white surface gleamed in the sun, and Cara could see black and pink flecks of color under the polished surface.

"Be very careful with them," cautioned Leolin. "They take a long time to make, and they aren't very easy to replace."

George looked up curiously. "How do you write on them?"

Leolin reached into his robes again and withdrew two thick twigs. "With these." He handed the twigs to Cara and George. Cara looked at the utensil carefully.

"What are these?" George asked.

"Bark," Cara answered, spinning the tool between her fingers. "You carved bark from the Junga trees in the hills."

Leolin looked at her in surprise. "Yes, exactly. The bark is dried and treated with certain oils. When rubbed on the stone it leaves a red mark that can be wiped off with a little water. This allows apprentice priests to practice writing letters hundreds of times without wasting valuable parchment."

George stared at the strip of bark in his hand in amazement. Even Cara was impressed. Her father had never bothered to show her how the priests learned to write.

"We're going to start with some basic letters. I have to warn you though; reading is a completely different skill than writing. You may have seen these letters thousands of times, but writing them is very different. There is a lot of fine motor control that goes on between your fingers and the bark. Take your time, and don't worry if you mess up. You can always erase any mistakes."

George looked at Cara nervously. Cara ignored him and placed the bark on the stone, sliding it carefully across the polished surface. A thin dark red lined followed the tip, sharply contrasting with the white stone. Cara curved her hand and pressed harder, and the line thickened and grew darker, curving down after the carved bark. George watched her, then hesitantly followed suit.

"Try and write your name," Leolin prompted.

Cara finished the C and moved onto the A. Despite herself, she found writing exciting. The stylus glided smoothly over the marble, obeying her every touch. It reminded her of the games she used to play with her mother when she was little. They would draw patterns in the dirt with sticks, and then try to copy each other's drawings.

"This is hard," George grunted, leaning over his tablet with intensity and struggling with the bark. His elbows stuck out as he tried to get a different angle with the utensil.

Leolin sat down next to him and reached for the stylus. "Here, let me help you with that. You want to try and hold the bark between your index finger and your thumb, while resting it on your middle finger. That way you can bend your wrist to get different angles." He placed George's fingers carefully on the bark. "Watch Cara, she's got it down perfectly. See how the bark just slides along the stone?"

George shot a jealous look at Cara. She blushed, surprised. She couldn't remember the last time she'd been complemented on a job well done. It felt strange to be the model student.

"That's actually quite good, Cara," Leolin said, leaning over George to get a better look at her tablet. "Your coordination is excellent."

Cara looked down at her finished name. The four letters were a little wobbly, and the last A was definitely too small, but it was easily readable. Cara smiled proudly at her work. She looked over at George's tablet, curious, and then let out a derisive snort. George had completed most of his name, but it was mostly unreadable. The E and O were indistinguishable from one another, and the G was hardly recognizable as a letter at all. George gave her a nasty look.

"Don't be rude, Cara. Most people have a lot of difficulty with this at first." Leolin reached into his robes and withdrew a small Penlet with a dark red cover. He flipped it open to the first page, then turned it around for George and Cara to see. A large intricate pattern was drawn over most of the first page. Flowing loops and bold lines crisscrossed over the page, creating a familiar symbol.

"You all know the symbol of the Creator," Leolin began. "For the next fifteen minutes I want you to try and draw this on your tablets. I'll leave the page open so you can copy it from here. This is one of the many skills you'll need as a priest – the ability to faithfully reproduce what you see on paper."

Cara opened her mouth to argue, then closed it sullenly. There was no need to cause a commotion, and she kind of enjoyed the drawing anyway. She leaned over her tablet and set to work.

The Creator's symbol had a fairly complex design. Cara found herself erasing and redrawing several parts on multiple occasions. Instead of asking for water she merely spit on the edge of her shirt and rubbed it on the stone surface. George frowned at her and edged a little farther away from her on the bench, hunching over his tablet like a dunbee with a scrap of food. Leolin sat a little further down on the benches, eyes closed as he prayed to the Creator. Cara ignored them both, focusing completely on her drawing. For the first time in a long time, she actually found herself having fun. She was just putting the finishing touches on the inner circle when Leolin opened his eyes and stood up.

"Okay, your time is up. Let's see how your drawings turned out."

Chapter Eight

George jumped to his feet and handed the tablet to Leolin. "I think I did a lot better this time!" he exclaimed.

Leolin looked carefully at the tablet in front of him. "Indeed you did! Not bad at all, George. You put a lot of effort into this."

George beamed at the complement. Cara slowly handed her tablet to Leolin. She tried to act like she didn't care, but she couldn't help feeling apprehensive about her drawing. Was it any good? Would Leolin like it?

Leolin accepted the tablet and gazed at it. His face remained neutral, but his eyebrows lifted slightly.

"Cara…" he began. "Cara, this is amazing."

George leaned over, trying to get a look at the tablet.

Leolin looked up at her. "I've never seen a novice writer draw such a comprehensive image. You have an exquisite eye for detail!"

George caught sight of the tablet and his eyes widened. He looked at Cara with newfound respect.

Cara squirmed, embarrassed at the praise but pleased all the same. "Thanks," she mumbled.

Leolin looked back down at the tablet. "To think of the drawings you'll be able to accomplish when you're a fully trained priest. The Penlets you transcribe will be beautiful!"

Cara frowned. "But I don't want to be a priest."

Leolin looked up at her slowly. "Now is not the time to discuss that, Cara," he urged, eyes flickering towards George.

Cara glared at Leolin, ignoring his warning. "Why can't I just draw for fun? Why do I have to be a priest?"

Leolin shook his head sadly. "Talent like this shouldn't be wasted. The Creator gave you this gift for a reason – He wanted you to help spread His faith."

A deep anger began to rise inside of Cara. "The Creator didn't give me anything."

"Yes, He did. He gave you everything."

Cara clenched her fists. Of course Leolin would give all the credit to the Creator. It was always the Creator who got praised. "Maybe I'm just finally good at something. Did you ever think of that?"

"Of course you're good at something," Leolin said soothingly. "The Creator has made sure of that."

Cara could feel red hot blood pumping through her veins. She wanted to jump up and scream at him, to shake him so hard that he would have to believe her. It wasn't fair. *How could I have been so stupid? He's only here to turn me into a believer. Well he can't! I'll never believe.* This new resolution flew across her mind like a flock of iraa birds, the rain from their wings splashing on her fiery thoughts and calming the rage inside of her heart. *I'll never believe,* she repeated to herself. She took a deep breath and stared at the ground, focusing on the sensation of her breath to keep her words from spilling out again.

Leolin gazed at her, a worried expression etched across his brow. When he was sure she was calm enough, he picked up his little Penlet. "There is one more portion of the test. I will read aloud a section from the Penlet, and I would like you to complete the sentence, if you know it."

George, who had been anxiously watching the fight, brightened.

"I'll call on you one by one. Cara, we'll start with you." Leolin flipped to the middle of the Penlet and scanned the page, his finger running over the lines. He smiled suddenly, then cleared his throat and began to read.

"No death can frighten me. No horror can touch me. For I know that the Creator is..." Leolin paused and looked up expectantly.

Cara knew the verse well. It was a favorite of her father's. But the last thing she wanted to do was play Leolin's stupid little game. She shrugged and stared at the ground.

George raised his hand in the air, wiggling his fingers in excitement.

"Do you recognize it?" Leolin prompted. Cara shook her head. He sighed. "Very well. George?"

"...with me in all things, from life unto death."

Leolin smiled. "Good. Now let's try again, Cara." He flipped the pages slowly and stopped at another section. "Above all things, the Creator is love. His love creates a..." Leolin paused again and looked up at Cara. Cara avoided his eye contact and continued to stare at the ground as George began waving his hand in the air. After a brief pause, Leolin called on George again.

"…net that supports us in our times of greatest need and deepest sorrows." George looked quite proud of himself. Cara almost wanted to get the next one right to wipe the smirk off of his face, but that would mean giving in to Leolin.

George got the next one right too. And the one after that. After almost ten minutes Cara was ready to run back into the classroom. Anything was better than listening to Leolin and George quote Penlet passages back and forth at each other.

"Okay, that's all for today. Thank you very much for letting me test you today."

Cara jumped to her feet and strode towards the classroom door, thankful to finally be done.

"Please send out the next two students!" Leolin called after her. She ignored him. When she entered the classroom she silently slipped into her chair in the back of the room. Mr. Baynor acknowledged their return with a nod, and sent out two more students for testing.

Cara had trouble listening to Mr. Baynor's lecture. He was droning on about the significance of animals and how they were gifts from the Creator. As his lesson continued, pairs of students occasionally left and entered the room. Most came back with large smiles on their faces. Cara ignored them all. She began dreaming about the belknay eggs she ate at Bakinu's house. She smiled dreamily, remembering the tangy exotic flavor and smooth texture. If only she could tell Mr. Baynor what she had eaten. He would be so horrified!

Finally, the last pair returned to the classroom. Leolin followed them in and stood near the doorway, hands crossed politely behind his back. The lesson ended shortly after, and Mr. Baynor dismissed everyone thirteen and under. Cara rushed for the door, eager to get home. She tried slipping past Leolin, but he put out his hand and grabbed her shoulder before she could get through the door.

"Wait a moment, Cara. I just need a second with Mr. Baynor."

Cara reluctantly stayed by his side, watching with envy as her fellow students flowed out the door.

"Leaving already?" Mr. Baynor asked, stepping closer and looking at Leolin curiously.

"I was instructed to return as soon as I finished testing," Leolin responded. "I'll be back tomorrow with the results."

"Very well." Mr. Baynor glanced at Cara. "And before you go, I would like to know what your father had to say about the reprimand token I gave you, and why you were not in school yesterday."

Cara shrugged. "He punished me. I spent most of yesterday in my room, quietly reading the Penlet."

Mr. Baynor raised his eyebrow and looked at Leolin skeptically. Leolin nodded in confirmation. "Very well then. I trust your father has the matter under control. I hope you have learned your lesson?"

Cara shot Leolin an icy glare. "Oh yes, I know my father will be watching."

Mr. Baynor grunted, then turned to Leolin and bowed his head. "Thank you very much for coming. It was great seeing you again."

Leolin bowed back. "It was a pleasure. I'll see you tomorrow." He turned and strode out of the room. Cara followed him eagerly out onto the dirt road. The sun hung high in the sky, partly obscured by large clouds. The morning chill had long since passed, and the midday sun was busy baking the hard dirt path. Cara ignored the heat and began walking home quickly. Leolin matched her pace, walking next to her with his red robes swirling above the dry dirt.

"You have to be more careful," he said quietly, staring over the crops on either side of the path.

"What?" asked Cara, irritated.

"When you spoke out against becoming a priest. You don't want to give others the wrong idea about your faith. Not everyone is as understanding as your father."

Cara snorted. "Understanding is not the word I'd use."

Leolin sighed and gazed back over the crops. "The Creator's beauty is all around us. If you open your eyes to His work, then His presence will become clear to you."

Cara glanced over the tall rows of grain on either side of the pathway. "All I see is a bunch of plants."

"But it's much more than that. It's a gift from the Creator. He gave us this grain so that we may feed ourselves. He gave us the sun so that we may warm ourselves. He gave us the...."

"But how?" interrupted Cara. "The Penlet says that the world was created in seven days. How can all this be created that quickly?"

"The Creator is all powerful. He…"

"Then why didn't He make it all in one day? Or two? Come to think of it, most of the stories in the Penlet don't make any sense. How can an odenpom talk? How can a person live inside the stomach of a giant queechee? How can the world be drowned in water, and how could Hano survive on the back of an iraa bird for forty days?"

Leolin shook his head. "The how is not important. We don't need to understand the Creator's power; we just have to have faith in Him."

Cara looked at Leolin incredulously. "Not important? How could you say that? Asking how is one of the most important things we can do!"

"The only how I am concerned with is how to serve the Creator," Leolin responded calmly.

Cara gritted her teeth. It was impossible. How could he stay so blissfully ignorant? *I'll have to teach him a lesson – punish him for his tolerance.* She grinned suddenly as an idea blossomed in her head. All she needed was a little time alone…

She remained silent for the remainder of the walk back to the church, planning her little scheme. She returned her Penlet to her room and started performing her chores, but Leolin continued to follow her, quietly helping her organize the Penlets in the pews. She restocked old candles and cleaned dust off of the tapestries, all with Leolin's help. Afterwards Leolin insisted that she read some Penlet passages and talk about their meanings. Cara argued, she had studied the Penlet all day in school, there's no way she would study it all evening as well! But Leolin insisted, enthralled by the idea of more time with his precious

Penlet. Even during dinner Leolin remained by her side, watching her every move and offering encouraging tidbits about the Creator's love when appropriate. It wasn't until the sun set that Cara was finally able to shake him. After plenty of yawning she convinced him that she was going to bed early. He bade her goodnight at her door and then left, walking down the hallway in the direction of her father's office.

Cara stepped into her room and closed the heavy door softly. She closed her eyes and counted to twenty before slowly opening the door a crack. She squinted down the hallway, making sure Leolin was out of sight before stepping out into the corridor. Several sconces flickered on the walls, lining the tall stone corridor with rows of flickering lights. Cara swept down the corridor and stepped through a side passageway that led to the barn. She entered the lofty room and headed straight for the tool shelves. A variety of metal and wooden implements hung from dozens of pegs on the wall, each instrument carefully crafted by priests for animal care. She stood for a few moments, looking over her options. A broom with a particularly long wooden handle leaned to the side of the tool shelves. She grabbed the broom and strode out of the barn, surveying the dark fields with a slight frown on her face. Dark shapes stood across the yard. A few gentle pulses of light weaved between the shapes as various belknay navigated around the slumbering odenpom. Cara lifted her broom and stepped into the yard, heading towards the grassy fields to the left of the fence. Wenooski didn't usually hang out in the main yard near the odenpom – they were more solitary creatures, but they liked the food the priests put out for them.

Cara stepped over the fence and began waving the broom around as she walked slowly through the field. She clucked gently and called out, hoping to attract a nearby wenooski quickly. The longer she was out here the more likely she was to be caught. Not many priests came out after the sun set, but sometimes they did nightly checks on the animals.

A low croaking noise emanated from the darkness to her right. Cara spun around and squinted through the darkness. She saw nothing, of course. Wenooski were hard to spot. She took a tentative step in the direction of the noise and thrust her broom out, waving it back and forth. The side of the handle clanked against something hard, stopping abruptly in midair. Cara smiled. Invisible or not, wenooski weren't very good at hiding. They spent most of their time being invisible, but they seldom moved far. On the rare occasion you could see them, they were large and slow looking. An enormous pebbly shell covered a long leathery body with small beady eyes.

Cara felt her way around the wenooski until she was fairly sure she was positioned by its tail. She then prodded it gently and made more clucking noises. Croaking in protest, the wenooski began to lurch forward. Cara felt the hard lump in the air jerk away from her, and she could hear the swishing of the grass as the wenooski lumbered over it. After several minutes of careful urging, she managed to get the wenooski over the fence and into the barn. As she passed the tool shelf she glanced at the combs she used to groom the odenpom. As an afterthought she grabbed several large tufts of hair from the tines and stuffed them into her pocket.

She peeked into the corridor to make sure no one was there before cautiously leading the wenooski down the hallway. She giggled at the thought of being caught. They wouldn't be able to see who was in the hallway, but they were bound to trip over the wenooski's large shell if they tried to walk past it. Cara carefully led the wenooski to Leolin's room. She knocked softly before peering in. Leolin wasn't there – he was probably still talking with her father, reporting the test results from the students, as well as her behavior. She quickly prodded the wenooski into the room, feeling the hard shell as she moved it into the center of the chamber. After it was in position she started searching for Leolin's walking shoes. The shoes he walked to the school with had thicker soles then the ones he wore around the church. After a few minutes she found the shoes neatly tucked into a cabinet at the foot of his bed. She removed the odenpom hair from her pocket and stuffed a little into each toe of his shoes. With any luck he wouldn't notice the hair in the morning.

She stood back and observed her work. The room certainly looked empty. The wenooski was completely invisible in the room – Leolin would be totally surprised. She grinned and then carefully closed the door behind the animal. Tomorrow would be a good day.

Chapter Nine

The next morning Cara was actually excited when Leolin knocked on her door. She sprang up in bed and struggled to control her face when she opened the door.

"Cara," Leolin greeted, nodding to her. He held out a bowl of grain mash for her to eat.

Cara examined his face for some sign of anger or annoyance. His dark eyes were calm and sincere, as always.

"Did you sleep well?" Cara prompted, taking the mash from him.

"Very well, thank you," Leolin replied. Was that a slight glimmer in his eye? Cara couldn't be sure.

Leolin said nothing else as they completed her morning chores. Annoyed at his silence, Cara thought furiously for another prank to play on him. As she was leaving the barn, her eyes fell on a small instrument on the tool shelves – a small wooden whistle. She grabbed it and stuffed it in her pocket. Before leaving for school, she grabbed a heavy cloak from her closet – a thick one that was good at stopping rain.

It was a little overcast as they walked to school that morning. Cara waited until they were well on their way down the road before she snuck the whistle out of her pocket. When Leolin wasn't looking, she pulled it out and blew on it for a while. No sound came out. Or at least, no sound that they could hear. Leolin glanced over at her and Cara quickly shifted her hand to make it look like she was scratching her nose. When Leolin looked away again, she resumed blowing on the silent whistle. Before long, Cara could hear the familiar pitter patter of rain on the dirt road. There were iraa birds nearby.

The iraa birds swooped over their heads, attracted by the high-pitched whistle. Priests often used this trick to attract flocks of iraa birds, especially when they wanted rain during a drought. With every flap of their wings a large sheet of water fell from the sky, landing on the ground beneath the birds. Cara quickly tucked the whistle back into her pocket just as the iraa birds passed overhead. Leolin winced as a large splatter of rain hit him straight on the head. The thick hood to the cloak Cara was wearing protected her from the downpour.

For the next five minutes the birds wheeled overhead, dumping buckets of water down on the two travelers. Despite her preparations, Cara's shoes were drenched by the downpour. After it became apparent that there was no food for them to eat, the iraa birds flew off, heading north towards the church. She brushed the water off of her hood and lowered it, glancing over at Leolin to see how he faired. She smirked at the sight. Leolin was drenched from head to toe. His dark hair was flattened to his head, dripping water over his face and onto his shoulders. His robes were completely soaked, the red cloth turned a much deeper shade from the water. He blinked several times, clearing the water from his eyes, then silently began wringing his hair out. Cara's smirk slowly faded from her face. *How could he still be so calm? At least the odenpom hair is still in his shoes — his toes should start to hurt anytime now.*

The school's weathered wooden walls appeared over the fields of grain. Cara and Leolin entered the school, and Cara sat towards the back near one of the large windows on the left. Leolin promptly began conversing with Mr. Baynor, talking in hushed tones about the results from the previous day's tests. Mr. Baynor appeared slightly aggravated at Leolin's words, but Cara ignored them. Before long the classroom filled up with bright-eyed eager students, and Mr. Baynor led them through the morning prayer. As the class sat down again in their seats, Leolin took the front of the classroom.

"Good morning class," he said, beaming over their heads.

"Good morning Leolin," the class chorused back.

"Yesterday's tests went very well. I'm proud of how well you applied yourself to the tasks I assigned." The thirteen-year-olds and up all sat up a little straighter, the compliment going to their heads. "Unfortunately, not all of you can become priests. As you know, there is usually only one person per age group who is selected to join the clergy."

The class began shooting sidelong looks at each other. They had never really thought about it like a competition before.

Leolin cleared his throat. "I have selected six promising candidates from the students I tested yesterday. For the next several weeks I will tutor these students individually. Those that do well will have a greater chance of being selected as apprentice priests upon graduation from this school. And those that do exceptionally well may be allowed to graduate early to start their duties as an apprentice priest."

The class began to shift restlessly. Cara slumped lower in her seat. It was disgusting how excited everyone was for these tests. George, sitting a few seats in front of her, let loose a small squeal of excitement.

"Could the following students please come outside with me," announced Leolin, smiling kindly. "Kris, Athene, Navia, Pertwee…"

Four students, fifteen- and sixteen-year-olds, jumped to their feet eagerly, wide smiles across their face.

"…Taylor, and Cara."

Taylor, a burly fourteen-year-old, stood up and joined the older students. Cara remained in her seat, not quite believing.

Leolin smiled over the class and then swept out of the room, his long red robes trailing at his feet. The other five students scrambled to follow him out, nearly tripping over their legs in their haste. Cara continued to sit in her chair, numb to the world.

"Cara!" Mr. Baynor barked. "He called your name. Get out there now." She looked up, startled. An ugly expression was written across his face. She slowly stood up and stumbled towards the door. Various classmates who were not selected glared at her as she passed. Cara slipped through the door and into the morning sun. Her thoughts finally began to churn again as the sun beat down on her face. *Leolin selected me to be a priest. He thinks I'm talented…*she shook her head vigorously. *This wasn't an honor. It was a prison sentence.* For the next several weeks she would be forced to undergo more testing. The last thing she wanted was to be a priest, and she had to make that clear to him. *But you'll probably be allowed to draw some more,* a quiet voice pointed out from the recesses of her mind.

"Cara, are you coming?" Leolin called out from across the dirt clearing. Cara slowly walked over to the group of students and sat woodenly on the bench next to them. Leolin gazed at her for a second, making sure she wasn't going to have an outburst, before clearing his throat again.

"Congratulations," he began, surveying the six promising pupils in front of him. "You all displayed exceptional talent in yesterday's preliminary tests. Over the next several weeks you will complete more detailed tests and undergo some basic penmanship and service training. Not all of you will be selected to become apprentice priests – but` with any luck most of you will achieve that honor."

Taylor squinted in concentration. "So that means…we're the only ones in the class who can become priests?"

"Let's just say you have a leg up on your classmates." Leolin reached into his robe and handed three drawing stones to the students. "We only have three drawing tablets, so we'll have to break into small groups. Navia, Pertwee, Kris, I'd like you to start with me. We're going to learn the initiation prayer and discuss some of the deeper meanings behind the words. Athene, Taylor, Cara, you'll start with the tablets. I want you to get familiar with the tablet and the stylus. Play with shapes, get used to the idea of drawing. Today I want you to focus on innovation and imagination instead of mimicry. Draw anything you want. I'll check on your progress from time to time until we switch groups. Do you have any questions?"

Everyone shook their heads, and slowly migrated into the groups that Leolin had announced.

"Wonderful," said Leolin. "Let's get started then." He handed the drawing tools to Cara's group before leading the other group a few paces away. He began his lesson with them, his soothing voice murmuring in the background. Cara shifted her focus down to the smooth stone surface in front of her. She knew she should resist, tell Leolin that this was not what she wanted so another more eager student could take her place. But the empty white surface in front of her begged to be drawn on. She sighed and gave in, setting her stylus to the smooth surface and drawing.

For two hours her group practiced drawing on the stone tablets. The thick red lines danced across the gleaming white surface of the tablet, reproducing shaky but recognizable images from the students' imaginations. Cara drew an odenpom with wings soaring through the sky, several belknay riding scutney over mountains, and a queechee burning down the church. Leolin stopped by to examine their drawings. He frowned at the sight of the church with flames, but he didn't say anything. The other students were pretty good at drawing too. Cara could recognize classmates, several animals, and the schoolhouse in their drawings.

"We'll be switching groups soon," Leolin interrupted. "Finish up your drawings."

Cara hunched over her sketch of a giant belknay stepping on the school building. She turned the stylus on its side, using the flat edge to shade in the red paint on the sides of the crumbling building. A sudden flash illuminated her drawing, whiting out the scene. It seemed to come from the air all around her. Cara blinked and looked up in surprise, wondering what had caused the flash. Her classmates looked equally confused.

KRRIIICKKOOOOOM!!!

A huge peal of thunder crashed through the air, following the lightning. Cara nearly fell out of her seat, and Navia screamed. Even Leolin was startled at the noise, ducking quickly as if something was thrown at him.

"What was that?" whispered Taylor, breaking the shocked silence. Cara glanced up at the sky. A few wisps of striated white clouds were smeared over the empty blue expanse, but there was no hint of a thunderstorm. There was no rain, no clouds, and no storm. What had the lightning come from?

Another bright flash erupted from the sky, blinding the entire group as they stared at the open blue air. It was again followed by a deafening roll of thunder, tearing its way through the sky and splitting the air all around them. The door to the school house swung open, and a bewildered Mr. Baynor stepped out to look up at the clear sky. Leolin grabbed the hands of the two students near him and ran for the school house. Cara and the rest of the group followed him, sprinting to the relative safety of the classroom. Another flash of lightning and thunder reverberated around them as the students sprinted inside and clustered near the window, watching the skies outside in terror. Cara's initial surprise started to fade into curiosity.

"What's going on?" Cara asked, out of breath. No one answered. Several students around her made the sign of the Creator as they trembled in fear. The rainless lightning and thunder continued outside. Cara stepped away from the window and edged towards Leolin and Mr. Baynor. They stood slightly away from the windows, wringing their hands and giving each other nervous looks.

Cara stopped in front of them. "What's going on?" she repeated, staring directly at Mr. Baynor.

Mr. Baynor wrung his hands, avoiding her gaze and staring out the window.

"...the end of days is yet to come..." Leolin whispered fearfully. "...bright bolts of light will arc down from the heavens under clear skies..." his voice cracked and he stopped, unable to finish the passage.

Cara frowned. "The Dursturock isn't coming." Another large flash erupted outside and lit up the classroom, casting stark shadows against the walls before disappearing abruptly.

Mr. Baynor blinked nervously. "Maybe she's right. Lightning doesn't always come with rain. It could just be dry lightning."

Leolin shook his head, regaining his voice slightly. "Dry lightning requires clouds."

"How about heat lightning? They're also called bolts from the blue..."

"Possibly. But then we would see some sort of storm clouds on the horizon, and it's not that hot out today..." Leolin trailed off.

Cara shrugged. "Heat lightning is certainly more likely than the coming of the Dursturock."

Leolin gazed at her seriously, his brow knotted in worry. "I hope you're right." Another large crash outside made him jump slightly. He braced for the next flash of lightning, but it never came. A minute passed. Then two. The students began to whisper nervously. Mr. Baynor slowly walked to the door of the classroom and opened it. He stepped outside cautiously, the eyes of forty-eight children following his every move. He stood in the open dirt yard for a few minutes, slowly walking around and gazing at the sky with fearful eyes. Nothing happened. Finally, he snapped his eyes back to the schoolhouse and entered briskly, running a hand through his thinning black hair.

"Right," he announced, his voice wavering slightly. "The lightning seems to have stopped. I think it's best if we take the rest of the day off from school. Go home, check on your families, make sure everyone is okay. Class is dismissed."

Cara could hardly believe her ears. School was cancelled? She got to go home early? A wide grin erupted across her face. She was the only one smiling. The rest of the class gave each other nervous looks before slowly shuffling out of the room, white knuckles clenching their Penlets close to their bodies.

Cara slipped out the door and quickly passed her fellow students. Most of them threw nervous glances at the sky as they walked, but she looked up with curiosity. What had Mr. Baynor called it? Heat lightning? *It must be pretty rare. I've never seen it before...*

"Wait!" called out a voice. Cara groaned at the sound of feet as Leolin ran up beside her. "You need to wait for me," he panted. "Your father made it very clear that I should stay by your side."

"Oh please..." muttered Cara.

He looked around nervously. "And with all this excitement, it's best that I keep an eye on you. If the Dursturock is coming..."

"The Dursturock is NOT coming."

Leolin looked at her, eyebrows raised at her confidence. "What makes you so sure?"

"Because the Creator doesn't..." she trailed off. *Do I really want to get into this argument again?* She cleared her throat and restarted. "Does the Creator love us?"

Leolin blinked. "Yes."

"Does the Creator want to see us in pain?"

"No."

"Then why would He create the Dursturock, the end of days? Why would He allow His people to go through such tragedy?"

Leolin shrugged. "It is not my place to know the mind of the Creator. It says in the Penlet that the Dursturock came before during a time of darkness and despair, before we were enlightened by the knowledge of the Creator. It was in His caves that we learned about Him, and it was our faith in Him that drove the Dursturock away."

"So the Dursturock was a way to teach us about the Creator?"

"Yes, I suppose so."

Cara sighed heavily. "So then why would the Dursturock come again?"

Leolin thought for a moment before answering. "In the Penlet, Chalazion gave a warning. He said, *'be warned, good people, for the end of days is yet to come...in a period of peace and prosperity there will be a loss of faith and a loss of lives.'* Many of the priests believe that the Dursturock will come when people become unfaithful – that the Creator will need to remind us that

His is the only true way. I don't know if this is true, but what I do know is that the Dursturock will come again. Just as the Penlet fortells."

Cara snorted. "I thought the Creator loved us!"

"He does."

"Then why would He kill His own people? Just to punish some nonbelievers?"

Leolin shook his head. "I cannot claim to know the Creator's mind. I simply have faith that He has a greater plan. Our faith is often put through many trials."

"That doesn't make sense," Cara retorted. "He's supposed to be all knowing and all powerful. He knows exactly what we'll do in the face of these trials, so why even test us?"

Leolin was limping slightly. He shook his head in denial. "You're wrong, Cara. It is this life that defines us. It defines our faith, our being, and our souls."

Leolin stopped walking suddenly, frowning at his feet. He slowly bent over, removed his shoe, and reached into the tip with long slender fingers. Cara started to giggle before she clamped a hand over her mouth, stifling the sound. She watched him closely, hoping for an angry explosion. Leolin promptly withdrew the compressed lump of odenpom hair Cara placed there the night before. He stared at it for a long moment before swallowing slowly and throwing the hair on the ground. Wordlessly he removed the identical tuft from the other shoe, and then replaced them on his feet. He slowly straightened back up and stoically resumed walking, eyes fixed on the horizon.

Chapter Ten

When they finally reached the church, the grounds were abuzz with activity. Priests rushed through the hallways, delivering messages and carrying old books from room to room. A dozen or so villagers had appeared at the church. They knelt along the pews with heads bowed in prayer, seeking safety and comfort in the house of the Creator. The yard was also busy – apprentice priests were out in full force, performing an inventory of the animals while herding them all to the grassy area inside the fence. Cara slowly began to perform her chores, but she was distracted by the unusual commotion. Leolin also had a hard time focusing. His fears from earlier in the day were rekindled when he saw the worry lines on every priests' face.

"Leolin!" a passing priest barked suddenly. Leolin whirled to face him. "Report to the yard immediately."

"But..." Leolin stammered, "I have orders to..."

"I don't care what your orders were," the priest interrupted. "All apprentice priests are to care for the animals. You know the second sign... *and the Creator's gifts will be slaughtered in great numbers.*' It's your job to make sure that doesn't happen."

"Yes, yes, of course," Leolin murmured.

"Good." The priest glanced at Cara. "The High Priest would like you to stay out of the way tonight. Finish your chores, and then go to your room."

Cara shrugged. "Sure." Leolin nodded to her then scampered off in the direction of the yard. The priest was gone too, already rushing off to another important task.

Cara slowly began performing her chores. She made sure each praying villager had a Penlet nearby as she carefully replaced all the burnt-out candles in the sconces lining the main chamber. As she collected the tiny wax stubs, another idea blossomed in her head. Grinning, she began stuffing the candle stubs into her pocket instead of in the discard bin. Once her pockets were filled she slipped out of the main chamber, navigating through the corridors until she found Leolin's room. Priests swept up and down the hallway, but none paid her any attention. She casually opened the door and walked into his chambers, as if they were her own. The room was approximately the same size as hers, but it was more sparsely furnished. The bed was small and simple and the dresser was utilitarian at best. She walked around the room and removed every candle she could find, replacing it with the stubby ones from her pockets. She even replaced the backup pile of candles that he kept in a box on top of his dresser. She then walked back into the corridor and replaced the candles on either side of his doorway. She stepped back and examined her work, grinning widely.

A passing priest eyed her warily. She quickly shut Leolin's door and tried to look busy, marching down the hallway with her pile of candles towards the main chamber. The priest looked away, and she sighed with relief. She continued to the main chamber and put the good candles in the stock cupboard. While she was gone, another two or three villagers had appeared in the pews. One had a small child with her. They knelt near the back, eyes closed in fervent prayer. Cara sighed. With this many visitors, she would be responsible for making sure they all had bread and water during their stay. She grabbed the wicker basket containing the thick slices of bread and began to walk up and down the pews, silently offering the food to those who wanted it. She stared at them curiously as she worked. She recognized many of their faces, but some were unfamiliar to her. It was a small town, but some residents only came to mass on schooldays when she wasn't around.

After the rounds of bread, she navigated the rows with a pitcher of water and a goblet. Most waved off the water, but one older man with a shock of white hair drank quite deeply. He thanked her sincerely for her kindness, and blessed her in the name of the Creator. Cara couldn't help but feel uncomfortable. Everyone expected her to be so pious as the High Priest's daughter. She hated it.

For once, Cara was glad to have to care for her odenpom. The main chamber was starting to feel a little oppressive. She strolled into the yard and began grooming her odenpom. The animal was more skittish than usual. It kept side stepping nervously, eyeing the commotion at the barn with apprehensive eyes.

"Stop it," Cara muttered angrily, chasing it with the brush. "There's nothing to be afraid of. I just need to finish..."

The animal side stepped again and Cara missed her stroke, falling forward onto her hands in the dirty grass. She stood up, hands on her hips, and frowned at the odenpom.

"And how am I supposed to brush you?" she accused it, cocking an eyebrow at its long shaggy back. The odenpom swung its head to the side, avoiding her gaze.

Just as Cara was going to take a step forward and resume her grooming, another astoundingly bright flash lit up the air around her. A huge crash rent the air, the thunder reverberating her eardrums. She jumped, startled. The field was suddenly full of large lopsided boulders, with Cara standing alone in the center. She heard shouts of alarm from the direction of the barn. Leolin emerged from the doors and ran to her side, dragging her in the direction of the church. Unnerved, she let him lead her into the relative safety of the barn. Back in the yard a few belknay ran haphazardly between the boulders, running in no particular direction as they gave off alarmingly bright flashes of light. A few apprentice priests sprinted out into the yard and rounded them up, herding them towards the church. The lightning and thunder continued, lighting up the darkening sky with frightening flashes of power. Cara watched the scene from the wide door of the barn. Leolin stood beside her, wringing his hands at the sight of the lightning.

"When will it stop?" he whispered, staring at the sky with wide eyes.

Cara shrugged, trying to shake off her discomfort. "I'm sure it will stop soon. It only lasted a few minutes this morning."

Leolin shook his head. "But then it came back. This is it, Cara, this is a sign. The Dursturock…"

"No," Cara said firmly, standing a little straighter. "It's just a little strange weather. Nothing to be afraid of." Once she said it out loud it was easier to believe.

Leolin shook his head slowly, but didn't answer. The field of boulders lay silently in front of them, a testament to his grim thoughts.

The rest of the evening passed in a blur. The animals that could fit were ushered into the barn and fed. Most of the priests, including the apprentice priests, were summoned into various meetings. The frantic activity of the morning had turned into nervous energy. Priests sent furtive glances out the windows, and more than one apprentice priest dropped what they were carrying when a door closed a little too loudly. Even Cara found herself looking over her shoulder. *It's nothing,* she told herself repeatedly. *They're just getting worked up about the weather. The Dursturock doesn't exist, so there's nothing to worry about.* But the more everyone else worried, the more she had trouble staying calm.

It was a relief when it was finally late enough to go to bed. Most of the priests were ordered to sleep, while some stayed up and started a watch duty. Leolin saw Cara to bed before heading back to his own chambers. Cara had almost forgotten about her little prank, but she remembered as soon as Leolin blew out the candle in her room. She smiled, grateful for something more fun to think about besides the stress and worry of the priests. She waited for him to close the door before silently opening it again and following him down the corridor. She stood outside his room after he entered and placed an ear against the thin wall. A few moments passed. Cara could hear Leolin fumbling in the darkness, trying to light the stubby candles with the good one he brought in from the hallway. After a few failed attempts, and a couple stubbed toes, she heard him curse under his breath and a thump as he kicked the bed in frustration. She smiled widely, thrilled to have pierced his stoic exterior, then returned to bed and fell into a deep slumber.

Cara woke up surprisingly early the next morning. The room was still dark. She shivered slightly, the memory of the nightmare she'd had washing over her. She couldn't remember the details of her dream, but the absolute terror clung to her like a queechee curled tightly around her forearm. She stayed under the covers for a while, relishing the comfort and warmth of her bed, but despite the early hour was unable to fall back asleep. Before long a faint horizon line began to shine through the window. Soon the morning bells would start to toll, and it would be another long and boring day. Another day with Leolin following her around. *I hope more lightning happens,* she thought bitterly. *Anything to make the day more exciting.*

She eased out from under the covers and washed up, splashing some cold water on her face from the washroom. She changed out of her nightdress and shuffled along the corridor to the barn. The morning air was cool and refreshing, but still quite dark. The sun had yet to crest the horizon. As she selected the morning tools for her chores, she caught sight of two apprentice priests leaning against the bales of wheat near the barn entrance. They were hard to spot in the dawn, their red robes blending in with the long dark shadows in the barn. One was snoring heavily, his soiled red robes rising and falling with every tumultuous breath. Cara stifled a giggle. What was the point of watch duty when the watchers couldn't stay awake through their shift? She held up a brush and cocked it back behind her head, ready to throw it at the neglectful acolytes, but a thought stayed her hand. Better if a senior priest found them like this. That way they couldn't accuse her of lying. Cara smiled and tiptoed past them, stepping over their legs as she entered the yard. She glanced over the field, searching for her odenpom, and then froze at what she saw.

Bloody carcasses and bone fragments were strewn across the red tinted grass. A few boulders remained, but even they were fractured and broken with rubble scattered around the scene of carnage. The tattered remains of a scutney were spread just a few paces away from Cara's feet. Its empty brown eyes gazed at the sky. Not a single animal was left alive in the field.

Cara's mouth opened in surprise, but no noise came out. Her grip loosened on the brush, and the heavy wooden instrument fell on the floor of the barn with a loud jarring clatter. The two apprentice priests woke up with a start, blinking in surprise and flushing in embarrassment when they realized they had fallen asleep on the job.

"Sorry, I'm so sorry," one stammered, struggling to his feet and brushing the wheat off of his cheeks. His eyes fell on the grisly scene. His voice trailed off to a squeak, and his partner looked over to see what was amiss. He gasped in horror. Cara continued to stare at the yard, numb with shock, as the apprentice priests stumbled back from the scene and raced inside to warn everyone else.

Cara's mind slowly began to work again. *The animals…what happened? What killed them? The Dursturock…no, it can't be. It can't be real.*

There were noises coming from behind her. The door to the barn burst open and the High Priest strode through, his elegant white robes flapping behind him. He came to a stop next to Cara and surveyed the carnage in the yard. Cara slowly turned her head and gazed at her father. For the first time she could see true fear in his eyes.

"BACK!" he barked suddenly. "Everyone back inside!"

Pandemonium broke out. Everyone was rushing for the door, frantic to get back into the church. Cara had trouble moving, but her father grabbed her roughly by the collar and yanked her towards the door. She followed obediently. Before she knew it she was in the main chamber. Priests were scurrying left and right, jostling her out of her stupor. She fell into a pew and stayed there, reassured slightly by the strong wood beneath her. *This is real*, she thought steadily. *This isn't a dream. It's happening. Right now.*

"SETTLE DOWN!" The High Priest's voice was larger than life. He stood at the front of the chamber in the pulpit, hands raised in the air with eyes shining. An apprentice priest shuffled past Cara on the pew and sat next to her. A glance told her it was Leolin. His face was deathly pale, starkly contrasting with his black hair. Everyone quieted, slowly sitting down in the pews and looking up at their leader. Only when complete silence fell upon the room did the High Priest lower his arms.

"We must remain calm," the High Priest intoned from the front of the room. "Have faith in the Creator. His love will guide us. Let us pray."

Heads bowed down across the room and voices swelled in prayer.

"The Creator and His glory shine upon us all. Let His mercy light our way, His wisdom guide our hearts, and His love save our souls. His path is the one true path of salvation and redemption to deliver us from evil."

The tension in the room dropped as the familiar words washed over everyone's ears. Even Cara felt thankful for the prayer. It brought a sense of normalcy back to the world.

"What has happened is undeniable," her father announced, making eye contact with as many people as possible. "We all know the passage." He closed his eyes and recited from memory.

"...the end of days is yet to come...Bright bolts of light will arc down from the heavens under clear skies, and the Creator's gifts will be slaughtered in great numbers. An unearthly roar will echo through the heart of the land, and the people will know unbounded fear. The Dursturock will return."

Everyone shifted uncomfortably. Several priests near Cara began shaking in fear, and one priest began muttering to himself, reciting some sort of personal prayer. A few looked up at her father with desperate eyes, hoping for some word of comfort or help, hoping that he would tell them this was all some sort of cosmic joke. That this was all just a dream, and they would wake up soon to the normal life they all knew and loved. The High Priest opened his eyes and pronounced their sentence.

"The Dursturock is coming."

Chapter Eleven

A few gasps sounded in the audience. Anyone in denial could no longer pretend. If the High Priest said it was happening, then it was happening.

"The church is the Creator's home," the High Priest continued. "This is a place of safety and refuge. Remain calm, and pray to the Creator. His wisdom will guide us through this time. He has done so in the past, and He will do so again."

Heads started bobbing in agreement throughout the audience. The main doors to the front of the church opened and a straggle of townsfolk staggered in. They joined the priests in the pews, whispering with their neighbors to find out what was going on. From what Cara could overhear, it sounded like the animal slaughters were not isolated to the church. Iraa birds had been found dead on the side of the road, and a farmer's yard was covered in dead dunbee. One person, a frail older woman who ran the village inn, said her home had been burned down by the lightning strikes. More villagers began to flood into the main chamber.

The High Priest cleared his throat and began speaking again. "Villagers, I ask you to pray. Pray for our safety, and pray for the Creator's mercy. Apprentice priests, please make sure everyone is given food and drink. Could the priests please join me in the conference room? We will pray for the Creator's wisdom, and decide a course of action."

The room began to come alive with activity. The apprentice priests in their red robes handed out bread and water to everyone in the pews. The white robed priests followed Cara's father through a side door into the conference room.

"Stay here," Leolin whispered as he stood to join the apprentice priests.

An unexpected surge of anger coursed through Cara. She glared at him. "What's the matter with you? Why are you always so submissive?" She stood up abruptly.

"Where are you going?" Leolin reached for her arm to stop her.

Cara shook him off. "I'm going to the bathroom," she lied. "I don't think I need an escort there." She exited the row and ducked out of the main chamber, away from the watchful eyes of Leolin and her father. She began to pace in the corridor, her thoughts whirling furiously in her head. *The Creator isn't real. That means the Dursturock can't be real. This is all just a big misunderstanding. But the animals are all dead. So what killed them?* She stopped pacing. She would have to go outside and investigate. Was it an illness? The lightning? The image of the bloody field swam before her eyes. *Okay, maybe not lightning. Maybe a crazy person?* There was only one way to find out.

Cara turned around and headed for the door to the fields. The corridor was deserted – everyone was in the main chamber praying for the Creator's forgiveness. She threw open the door and paused in the frame, surveying the grisly scene in the yard.

She gulped, pushing down the feelings of panic, and then stepped out.

She headed north through the yard, looking straight ahead as she strode towards the fields behind the church. Her toe bumped against a crumbled rock on the ground, a remnant of what may have been her odenpom. She gulped and pushed forward, clenching her jaw and trying not to look at the carcasses strewn around her. She made it to the fence and quickly ducked under, continuing her fast pace into the deserted fields beyond the yard. Eventually she began to slow down and look around. There were fewer bodies on this side of the fence, but there were several stray bones and tufts of fur littered across the grass. She glanced back behind her, and was surprised to see the distance she had put between herself and the church. A crunch sounded from the ground. Cara jumped, surprised, and realized it was a bone. She knelt down and picked it up. The bone gleamed white in the weak morning sun. A few threads of meat hung off of the end, and there was blood smeared along the shaft. Cara noticed that there were also long deep gouges in the hard surface of the bone. She ran a finger over the scratch. It was very deep and rough to the touch. *What could have caused this?* she wondered, holding the bone up to the light.

"Cara!" a voice shouted. Cara dropped the bone and whirled around, her heart racing in her chest. Bakinu waved, hurrying towards her. His thin face was flushed red from exertion, and his queechee Cheea swayed precariously on his shoulder.

"Bakinu?" Cara blurted out, astonished.

The old man caught up to her, smiling but slightly out of breath. "It's great to see you again so soon, Cara." The smile slid off of his face. "I only wish it was under better circumstances."

"What are you doing here? I thought you were exiled…"

A tired look appeared in Bakinu's eyes. "I wouldn't have come if the situation wasn't so desperate. My house was burned down by lightning and my belknay were slaughtered during the night. I didn't know what else to do. I need help."

"I don't know how we can help," Cara replied. "Our animals were slaughtered too. Most of the village is sitting in the church right now, praying for help from the Creator."

Bakinu looked past her and noticed the bloody bones scattered across the field for the first time. "No…" he whispered. "I didn't think…but I saw an odenpom a few miles back."

"Really?" Cara said, eyebrows shooting up in surprise. "I guess…some must have gotten away. From the bodies, it looks like most were slaughtered."

"Was anyone hurt?"

Cara shook her head. "Just the animals. Everyone thinks it was the Dursturock." She looked at Bakinu and tentatively smiled, hoping for some sort of consolation, a reassurance that all this religious talk was nonsense and everything was going to be okay. Bakinu didn't return the smile.

"But it can't be the Dursturock," Cara blurted out, her heart sinking in her chest. "The Creator doesn't exist, so how can the Dursturock?"

Bakinu shrugged. "I just don't know anymore, Cara. I don't have all the answers. The truth is I'm just as scared as you are."

The words were like a slap to the face. Cara blinked, stunned, her last refuge ripped away from under her feet. *If Bakinu isn't sure, how can I be? Does the Creator actually exist?*

"Cara!" another voice shouted, this time from behind. Cara and Bakinu turned to see an apprentice priest jogging in their direction, red robes flapping behind him.

"Leolin…" Cara muttered, the usual sense of irritation returning.

"Who is he?" asked Bakinu, curious.

"He's the babysitter my father assigned to me after I ran away," explained Cara. "I thought I lost him back at the church."

Leolin caught up with them, breathing heavily. "Cara…" he huffed. "We need…to get back…right now!" He glanced over his shoulder, as if afraid a monster would appear at any moment.

"Why?" she challenged, irritated at his tone.

"Because of…the Dursturock!" he exclaimed, flailing his arms wildly at the surrounding air.

Cara crossed her arms over her chest. "Maybe I don't…"

"Cara," Bakinu interrupted. "I would like to go to the church too."

Cara spun around and stared at him. "You what?"

Bakinu stared back gravely. "I came here for protection from whatever slaughtered my belknay. I don't know if it was the Dursturock or not, but what I do know is that there's safety in numbers. We should go back to the church."

Cara stared at him wordlessly. Her emotions were a whirl-wind, mostly telling her to yell and scream at the old man, but her common sense overruled them.

"Are you the exiled one?" Leolin interjected, giving Bakinu and his queechee a wary look.

"Yes."

Leolin shook his head. "Then you can't come back to the church. The priests won't allow it."

"What?" exclaimed Cara. "How could you say that? He's desperate!"

"I'm sorry, but exile is forever. He knew that when he denied the Creator."

"But…"

"Cara," Bakinu interrupted, placing a hand on her shoulder. "It's okay. I suspected this might happen, but I thought it was worth a try."

Cara glanced between the two, a frown on her face. "No, it's not okay. If Bakinu can't go back to the church, then neither will I."

"Cara!"

Cara crossed her arms and glared back at Leolin. He stared back for a moment, a frown on his face, before sighing and looking at the ground. "Fine," he muttered. "As long as you come back to the church right now."

Cara nodded and grabbed Bakinu's hand, pulling him with her towards the church. Leolin looked at the old man nervously before following, eyes darting around the yard. The group trekked through the open fields, stepping carefully to avoid the bones littered throughout the grass. Within several minutes they had crossed the fence and entered the main yard of the church. The old man's eyes widened as he saw the carcasses strewn across the yard. Cara started to lead the group in through the back door to the church, but Leolin threw out an arm to stop Bakinu.

Cara whirled around angrily, "He's coming in, or I'm staying out here."

"Yes," Leolin answered, "but the queechee is not coming in."

Bakinu paused and then nodded reluctantly. "Yes, of course." He offered his forearm to Cheea, and she readily climbed onto it. He then raised his arm to the sky and made a pushing gesture, whistling as he did so. Cheea jumped and spread her wings, soaring up into the sky with several strong beats. Bakinu watched her fly away with worried eyes.

"Now hurry," Leolin whispered, pushing Cara into the doorway of the church. Luckily there was no one in the corridor to note their return. The group slipped back into the main chamber and slid into an empty pew. Cara looked around the room in surprise. It looked as if the entire village was in the church. There were very few open pews, and the apprentice priests were nearly out of bread and water. Leolin slid next to her on the pew and stayed uncomfortably close to her. She glared at him, but he ignored her gaze, determined to not let her out of his sight again.

Most of the villagers in the room had their heads bowed in fervent prayer. Leolin joined them, but Cara stubbornly kept her chin up. She glanced over at Bakinu. He looked very much out of place. His eyes darted nervously around the room, and he was paler than usual. The soaring ceiling arched high above his head, and his neck strained as he looked up at it.

"You okay?" she asked kindly.

Bakinu smiled weakly. "It's been more than thirty years since I sat in this room, but it still looks the same. How could time have passed so quickly?"

A family in the pew in front of them was quietly praying. The oldest woman, presumably the mother, turned around at Bakinu's words. She gazed at him for a moment, frowning, then her eyes widened with recognition.

"It's so beautiful," Bakinu sighed, still talking to Cara. "I'd forgotten just how breathtaking this room was."

The older woman slowly stood up and squeezed through the pews, heading towards the front of the room. She stopped a passing apprentice priest and whispered to him, eyes wide as she pointed at Bakinu in the pews. The young man looked alarmed and ran off towards the conference room.

"Bakinu," Cara whispered loudly. "I think we may be in trouble."

A few minutes later, the High Priest emerged from the meeting room. The apprentice priest pointed at the pew Cara was sitting in, and her father frowned. He swept across the room and approached the pew, white robes swirling over the stone floor. Bakinu started to stand, but Cara pulled him down. Leolin lifted his head, and his eyes went wide when he saw the High Priest walking towards them.

The High Priest came to a stop next to the pew. He gazed at his daughter seriously before turning to address the old man.

"Bakinu, if I'm not mistaken?"

The old man nodded, his eyes full of fear.

"I'm afraid I'm going to have to ask you to leave."

Cara started to stand, indignant. "Why should…" her sentence was cut off when Leolin yanked her back down to the pew. His worried face and her father's angry glare silenced her.

"I realize the situation I've put you in," started Bakinu, gazing at his feet, "but I come before you a humbled man. My house has been destroyed and my animals slaughtered. I am helpless." He slowly looked up at the High Priest, his eyes moist. "I beg for your forgiveness, and for your help."

A crowd began to gather around the pew. Villagers watched with interest, scowls on their faces and anger in their eyes. Whispering started among the villagers at Bakinu's words, but they stopped when the High Priest started talking.

"I am sorry for your plight, but I cannot forgive your transgressions. You have denied the Creator from your heart, and so he exiled you from his home. Allowing you to stay is to disobey the Creator."

Heads nodded from all around. One villager yelled "yeah," and another added "you don't belong here!"

Bakinu trembled in fear. "I have nowhere else to go…" his voice trailed off, and he swallowed the lump growing in his throat.

"We cannot help you," responded the High Priest, "especially in this time of crisis. You must leave." His face was stern, but there was sorrow in his eyes. *At least he has the humanity to look pained,* Cara thought bitterly.

"This is your fault!" a shrill voice screamed from the audience. Cara looked up and saw the older woman who had noticed Bakinu earlier. Her eyes bulged slightly from her face, features contorted into an ugly grimace. She pointed at the old man, her finger shaking slightly. "'*In a period of peace and prosperity there will be a loss of faith and a loss of lives.*' It's you! Your loss of faith has brought the Dursturock down upon us!"

Bakinu winced at her words. "I'm sorry…" he whispered. The audience ignored his plea, shouting out against him.

"Get him out of here!"

"How dare he show his face…"

"Shame on you…"

"He should die…"

"Kill him!"

The High Priest rested his hand on Bakinu's shoulder. "Leave now, Bakinu. You are not welcome here."

Bakinu rose shakily to his feet.

"No," Cara started to protest, but Leolin clasped a hand over her mouth. Villagers continued to shout as Bakinu slowly slid past Cara and exited the pew. A shoe flew through the air and narrowly missed the old man's head. Cara ripped Leolin's hand away from her mouth, but he clasped the other one over it and held her in the pew as she struggled to stand. The crowd parted reluctantly for the old man as he stepped slowly through their ranks. He headed towards the back door, flinching at every insult and jibe that flew his way.

"TTTTHHHHHHUUUUUURRROOOOOAAAAAAW WWWWWWRRRRRR!"

A piercing, terrifying, distinctive roar ripped through the air, silencing everyone. The thunderous baritone reverberated through the room, resonating with high pitched keening notes that stilled the heart of every person in the church. The Dursturock had come.

Chapter Twelve

Everyone froze. The roar lingered in the air, vibrating the stones in the walls.

There was panic.

Mayhem.

Shoving.

Fighting.

Chaos

Screaming.

Walls caved in, bright light shining.

Pain.

Blood.

Tears.

RUN. RUN. RUN.

More screaming.

Frantic pushing.

Bodies on the ground.

Terror waiting behind.

RUN RUN RUN.

Grass was flattened underfoot.

Air whisked tears off of faces.

Legs aching, heart aching, lungs burning from

pain.

Footsteps melded with the sound of panting, a

steady drum of terror.

RUN. *Keep on running.* Got to get away.

Cara gasped for breath. *Run, just run. Where though? Where are we running?*

Bright sunlight spilled over Cara, warming her overheated body as she sprinted through the fields. She knew she had to run, but where or why was unimportant.

Someone bumped against Cara, causing her to stumble briefly. She looked around her, suddenly aware of the people running on either side of her. She was startled to notice that there were dozens...no, over a hundred, people running with her. Most of the village, in fact. She started to slow down, but the crowd wouldn't let her. She kept on running, panting, trying to keep up with everyone. She noticed Leolin running nearby. She reached out, touching his shoulder, breathing too heavily to call out his name, but he didn't seem to notice her. His face was glazed over with fear. She looked at the other villagers and noticed that they too were unfocused, as if they were unable to think. *What's going on?* She could remember....nothing. Just panic and fear. They were in the church, and then there was that noise... She glanced around at the other villagers. Some were aware, like her, but most were still in a trance, running for their lives.

A few minutes later, the pack began to slow down. Villagers started to look around, confused. Finally they all slowed to a jog, and then a few minutes later they came to a stop. Leolin blinked, confused, and looked around. Cara sat down abruptly, limbs weak from exhaustion. A painful stitch had developed in her side and she grabbed it, wincing in pain.

"Where are we?" someone asked, looking around in a daze.

Leolin blinked and gazed at the horizon, trying to get his bearings. "I think...I think we're north of the church."

Cara looked back and saw the church in the distance, several miles away. They had run into the hills surrounding the valley. Some villagers were frantically looking for their families, while others were tearfully reuniting with their loved ones. Everyone was asking questions.

"I can't remember…"

"What happened…"

"Did you hear that roar?"

Everyone stopped talking as they remembered the sound. Several villagers made the sign of the Creator at the memory.

"The final sign…" whispered Leolin. "'*An unearthly roar will echo through the hearts of the land, and the people will know unbounded fear.*'"

Cara blinked back tears. *How is this possible? The Dursturock…it's real?*

"CARA!" a desperate shout caught her attention. The crowd parted readily for the High Priest as he ran to his daughter. He embraced her tightly, hugging her to his chest. Cara hugged him back, thankful for once to find something normal and secure.

"Are you okay?" he asked, pulling back and looking her in the face. Cara nodded shakily. He hugged her again tightly and then kissed her on the forehead before standing up and facing the crowd.

"Gather around," he bellowed. The villagers started to form a circle, frightened faces lining the crowd. There were at least a hundred villagers there, but many were missing. Many tear-stained lonely faces dotted the crowd amidst reunited families holding hands.

"Does anyone remember what happened?" the High Priest intoned. Most people shook their heads, confused. A few people murmured something about a roar, but nothing more.

The High Priest raised his hand for silence. "With the final prediction come to light, the prophecy is completed. The Dursturock has come."

"What are we supposed to do?" a plaintive voice cried from the crowd.

"We aren't safe here," the High Priest answered, "and the church has likely been destroyed. We must find a place of shelter, a place to survive the Dursturock."

"What about the sacred caves?" Leolin stepped forward from the crowd. A thin trail of blood was smeared across his cheek from a cut beneath his left eye.

The High Priest raised an eyebrow. "The caves?"

Leolin shifted nervously. "They aren't far from here. The Penlet teaches that our ancestors took shelter from the Dursturock there. Maybe we should too."

The Head Priest smiled weakly. "Yes, of course. Thank you Leolin." He raised his voice so the entire crowd could hear him. "We head for the sacred caves. We must move quickly, before we lose any more people."

Murmurs of assent rippled through the audience. The High Priest stepped through the crowd and led the villagers northeast, heading towards a particularly steep hill bordering the valley. Cara followed her father, staying one step behind him as they walked briskly towards the hills. Leolin shadowed her, unsure of what to do now that she was so close to her father.

It took the villagers nearly thirty minutes to reach the caves. They kept up a quick pace, driven by fear, but some of the people had trouble keeping up. Cara noticed more than one sprained ankle starting to swell. Her own legs were tired, burning and aching quite strongly. She looked down and was startled to see thin scratches and smears of blood on her calves. Try as she might, she couldn't remember how she got them. The group began to murmur slightly when they could see the cave in the distance. Cara watched numbly as the rocky entrance grew larger and larger, the narrow slit overshadowed by a low ledge of wild grass. Cara's mind was sluggish. All she could think about was the Dursturock. *How could this happen? If only Bakinu was here, he might be able to explain this.* She gasped. *Bakinu! Did he survive?*

"The Caves of Chalazion…" Leolin's voice whispered.

Cara looked around to see Leolin walking next to her, eyes fixated on the opening in the caves ahead.

"I've been looking forward to seeing these caves my entire life," he continued, slightly breathless. "Now I may never have an initiation ceremony. But at least I'll see the caves."

Cara ducked as they entered the cave, her head narrowly missing the hard rocky shelf. She shuffled forward, bent over awkwardly as she followed Leolin through the corridor. The rock lining the walls was black with a smooth shiny surface, reflecting the light from the outdoors well into the entrance. After a few minutes, the ceiling opened up and the walls fell away to either side. Cara straightened and looked around, her eyes widening at the sight.

The cave was huge. A massive chamber arched high above her head, shimmering in the reflected light of candles placed throughout the cavern. Priests scurried along the edges, lighting the candles as she watched. Their white robes shone against the black cave walls. Cara noticed a soft noise in the background.

She squinted through the dim light and noticed a little stream running through the center of the chamber. It was fed by multiple trickles of water funneling down from cracks in the walls. The polished black rock was covered with moisture, enhancing the reflections of light throughout the chamber. The cavern was clearly carved out in some places. The floor was smooth and level from years of tender care, and the stream was bordered with engraved rock. There were small trickles of water artistically circling the cave, strategically placed near rows of candles to reflect the light. Upon closer examination Cara noticed gaps in the walls. Other chambers lay adjacent to this one, the small openings connected in series.

Cara was so captivated by the view that she walked straight into something solid. She staggered and grabbed onto Leolin, who struggled to keep his balance. She blushed, embarrassed. A large stalactite and stalagmite met in the middle to form a thick black pillar, which she had walked straight into.

"You okay?" asked Leolin.

Cara nodded. "Yeah, no harm done." She looked around the cave in wonder. "It's…beautiful. What kind of rock is this?"

"Obsidian," sighed Leolin. "It's extremely rare. As far as I know, it only exists in these caves. I had heard it was beautiful, but I never could have imagined this."

"Villagers!" bellowed a voice. Leolin snapped his head around. The High Priest was standing on a thick stalagmite with a flat top. Everyone in the room stilled and listened.

"These are the sacred Caves of Chalazion," he announced. "Our ancestors used this place as shelter from the Dursturock, and we shall do the same. The Creator will watch over us and give us strength to survive."

"How long will we be here?" shouted out a worried voice from the crowd.

The High Priest frowned. "As we know from the ritual of Remembrance, our ancestors lived here for fourteen years before the Dursturock passed and the land was safe to return to."

Murmurs swept through the audience. People shuffled nervously, frightened at the prospect of a future in this strange place.

"We need to be strong!" the High Priest shouted. "The Creator will lead us through this difficult time." He turned to a collection of priests to his right. "We must first establish our situation. Clergy, I need you to perform an inventory of the food, water, and candles. Report back within the hour. We also need to account for people. Perform a headcount. How many did we lose? Do we have any wounded? Please see to their medical needs."

The priests nodded and scurried off, frantically rushing to obey the High Priest's orders. Leolin and the other apprentice priests stood about awkwardly, unsure of how to perform their duties. Within minutes a priest appeared at Leolin's elbow.

"You two," he barked. "Follow me." He spun around and marched towards one of the doorways in the cavern wall. Leolin glanced at Cara before following him. Cara walked behind the two clergymen, observing the opulence of the cave as she passed under the high craggy ceiling. The smooth polished walls of the cave became rough and jagged as they rose higher towards the ceiling, the natural shapes of the rocks emerging from the cavern edges.

The older priest passed into a side passage in the wall, carrying a lantern in front of him. The corridor twisted and came to an abrupt end with several small hollows carved into the wall. Each hollow was stuffed full of old robes, some faded and worn, and others with holes in them.

"Here," the older priest said brusquely, shoving a heap of rags in Leolin's arms. "Use these and some water to wash off some of the blood on the villagers." He glanced at Cara. "You too." He grabbed a pile of rags for himself before striding back down the corridor. Cara and Leolin hurried to keep up with him, anxious to stay in the circle of light the lantern cut out of the darkness. Within moments they were back in the main chamber, the black walls soaring far above their heads.

Leolin handed a small pile of rags to her. "Here. You can get started on the left side of the room; I'll take care of the right."

Cara promptly dipped one of the rags in the tiny rivulet of water running down the wall and dabbed it on Leolin's forehead. He jerked back, surprised, and then smiled weakly when he saw the smear of blood on the rag. She finished cleaning his wound and then walked away wordlessly, heading towards the other side of the cavern.

Many of the villagers were sitting down on the cold stone ground, huddled near their families. Cara numbly walked from person to person, washing blood off of frightened faces and cleaning both shallow and deep wounds. Most cuts were no longer bleeding, but a few were still oozing. To these she applied a clean rag and asked them to keep pressure on the wrap for a while. There were many cuts and scratches from simple abrasions, several sprained ankles, swollen wrists from falls, and dozens of dark, angry bruises that seemed to grow as she cleaned them. As she helped the villagers her gaze fell over familiar and unfamiliar faces, including several older farmers, some younger classmates, and even Mr. Baynor. It was while helping him that she noticed something unusual.

"How did you get this?" she asked, staring at his cut while carefully removing the dried blood around it.

Mr. Baynor winced, clearly uncomfortable with Cara as a nurse. "I don't remember," he murmured, looking away from the gash on his leg.

The wound was long, deep, and very straight, quite unlike any of the other superficial cuts in the room. It reminded her of the cut John had received from Cheea when she was defending Bakinu, except much larger.

"It's almost like an animal…" she trailed off. She remembered the long deep scratches on the bones of the dismembered odenpom. Those also looked like animal scratches, come to think of it.

"Animal?" Mr. Baynor scoffed. "That's impossible. All the animals were killed when the Dursturock came."

Cara ignored him, her mind racing. Animal scratches on the odenpom, animal scratches on the villagers. If an animal attacked the odenpom, then that means it wasn't the Dursturock. She gasped, dropping her rags in astonishment. *The Penlet was wrong. The Dursturock isn't the end of the world, it's an animal!*

Chapter Thirteen

"What?" Mr. Baynor asked, annoyed.

She stood up, oblivious to his presence. Of course the Dursturock was an animal. How could she have been so stupid? The odenpom were eaten, just like a queechee would eat a dunbee.

"Are you even listening to me?" Mr. Baynor said, raising his voice and holding up the rags she dropped. "You have a job to do, so do it! Pick up these rags immediately!"

Cara turned from him and walked away in a daze. It was hard to wrap her head around it. She had assumed that if the Creator didn't exist, then neither could the Dursturock. But the Dursturock did exist – it just wasn't what people thought it was. Could the same thing be true for the Creator? She gazed over the people in the cavern, stunned by this new revelation. Villagers peppered the cavern floor, sitting in small groups and whispering quietly to one another, all oblivious to her thoughts. An older man sat by himself off to a side, the candlelight reflecting off of his balding head. She blinked. *Bakinu?*

Cara nearly tripped over her legs as she rushed over to the old man. Bakinu looked up as she approached, startled by the noise, and smiled weakly when he recognized her.

"You're okay," he whispered. "I couldn't find you in the crowd. I thought you had…" the smile slipped off of his face.

"I thought you were dead," Cara said bluntly, kneeling down and hugging him tightly. "Where's Cheea?"

The old man blinked back tears. "I don't know."

"I bet she lived," reassured Cara. "She was flying north of the church when the attack came."

"I overheard a priest saying that 96 people were missing," Bakinu said solemnly. "To think, 96 lives gone in the blink of an eye…"

"All gone because of you."

Cara and Bakinu looked up, startled. Cara was stunned to see Leolin gazing down at them, an unusual glint of anger in his dark brown eyes.

"Leolin!" Cara admonished. "This isn't his fault."

"Isn't it?" Leolin asked, his voice icy. "The Dursturock only arrived once this heretic entered the Creator's church and defiled His home."

Bakinu hung his head in shame. Cara stood up angrily. "Then it would be my fault too," she growled. "I'm just as much of an atheist as he is."

Their argument was starting to attract some looks from nearby villagers. Seeing this, Leolin grabbed Cara and Bakinu and dragged them across the chamber and through a small doorway in the cavern wall, grabbing a lantern as he left. They passed down a narrow shimmering corridor and took the first left into a large hole in the wall. The hole emerged into a cozy little room, stuffed from floor to ceiling with blankets and stone cutting tools. Bakinu sank to the ground as soon as Leolin released his arm, sitting between two large piles of blankets. Leolin whirled around to face Bakinu, the scowl on his face deepened by the flickering light of the lantern he held.

"So what do you plan on doing to us?" Cara challenged him.

"You," he pointed at Cara, "stay out of this."

"No!" Cara yelled. "I'm just as much in this as Bakinu is."

"You can't honestly tell me you still doubt the Creator's existence."

Cara lifted her chin in defiance.

Leolin's eyes narrowed. "The signs of the Dursturock happened, just as the Penlet predicted. The Dursturock appeared, just as the Penlet predicted. And now we are taking shelter in the sacred caves, just as the Penlet predicted. It's obvious that the Penlet is the word of the Creator. What more could you want?"

"Cara…" Bakinu's soft voice cut off Cara's angry retort. "He's…he's right. I never thought I'd say it, but the Dursturock is real. The Creator is real. How else could all of this happen? The Creator is punishing us for our disbelief. It is a miracle that we're still alive."

"A miracle?" Cara asked, incredulous. "What kind of a miracle kills 96 innocent people? If this was truly a punishment from the Creator for not believing, then shouldn't we have been the first to die?"

Bakinu fell silent again, unwilling to argue with Cara. His shoulders drooped downwards and his lip trembled in fear. For the first time Cara noticed his age instead of his energy. His graying hair clung in wisps around the bald spot on the top of his head, and his arms and legs looked thin and frail. Cara felt a sudden surge of pity for the old man.

"You...you have repented?" Leolin's voice broke the silence, softer than before. He gazed curiously at the old man, a hint of the familiar kind expression returning to his face.

"Yes." Bakinu gazed up at him from the floor. "I was wrong. The Creator does exist. I am ashamed that so many lives were lost in teaching me this lesson."

Cara stepped back, stunned. "How...how could you say that?"

Bakinu blinked back tears. "The young man is right, Cara. My scorn for the Creator brought on His wrath."

"But you said that there was no Creator!"

Bakinu shook his head, speaking softly. "And I was wrong. The coming of the Dursturock is undeniable proof. The Creator exists."

Leolin stepped closer to the old man and placed his hand on his shoulder, kneeling next to him. "You have come a long way," he murmured. "The Creator has shown His wrath, but He is also capable of great love. He never gives up on His people."

Bakinu gazed at Leolin. "He would forgive me?"

Leolin smiled kindly. "The Creator is love. If your heart is truly full of sorrow, if you truly seek redemption, then the Creator will welcome you with open arms. The path to redemption always begins with introspection."

"Seriously?" Cara exclaimed. "You actually believe all of that crap?"

Leolin ignored her.

She put her hands on her hips. "The Dursturock isn't the end of the world. It's an animal."

Leolin blinked, confused. "An animal? Why would you say that…"

"All the bones," she continued, "have slashes in them. Like an animal ripping apart its prey. And the odenpom. There were large parts missing, like some animal ate a few bites and left."

"That doesn't mean…"

"And some of the villagers have the same claw marks."

Leolin cocked an eyebrow at her. "And I suppose the roar was actually a literal roar from this animal?"

Cara gasped, the realization hitting her like a slap to the face. "Yes, you're right! Of course!" She beamed at Leolin, a wide grin plastered across her face. "If the Dursturock is an animal, then it would have to have powers!"

"That doesn't make any…"

"Think about it," Cara interrupted, her thoughts jumping around like the dry lightning in the sky yesterday. She turned from Leolin, pacing back and forth across the storage room. "After that roar we remembered nothing. Just fear and panic. So why can't the roar be its power? A magical roar that inspires overwhelming fear. So powerful that it overrides thought, rational behavior, even memory!"

Leolin frowned. "We were frightened. It's not unusual to experience memory loss in periods of extreme terror."

"All of us?" Cara asked. "All of us losing our memory at the same time? You heard the roar. It was more than just fright – it was overwhelming, inexplicable fear. It was a magical power."

"Even if the Dursturock is caused by a creature, so what? The Creator used it to bring the Dursturock."

Bakinu, who had been watching Cara very closely, slumped over at Leolin's words. "He's right, Cara," he sighed, defeat in his eyes. "The Penlet still predicted the coming of the Dursturock."

Cara's eyes widened, a new thought blossoming inside her head.

"It's happened before…" she stammered. "This is the second time…"

"What are you talking about?"

"What if…" she swallowed eagerly. "What if the Penlet isn't a prophecy? What if it's a history?"

Leolin and Bakinu stared at her blankly, not following. Cara sat down abruptly on a nearby stack of blankets, her voice growing stronger as the pieces started falling into place.

"Imagine our ancestors, hundreds and hundreds of years ago. The Dursturock, a dangerous magical animal, attacks and spreads chaos and fear. Our ancestors find these caves and hide here. It takes years before they gain enough courage to leave. When they do they find the animal has moved on. They aren't able to remember what caused the pain and suffering, so they create a story. They imagine the Creator, the Dursturock, the Penlet, everything! All as a way to warn future generations in case it happened again."

Leolin shook his head. "Cara…"

Bakinu placed a hand on Leolin's arm, gazing at Cara with wonder. "Wait, let her finish."

"The lightning, the animal deaths, the roar…these were all signs that they remembered, and so they were signs that they could warn us about. But over time the purpose of the Penlet was distorted. Amendments were made. The book became more about worshiping the Creator and less about the Dursturock." She looked up and clapped her hands together. "It fits! Don't you see? The Creator doesn't exist!"

Bakinu slowly pushed himself to his feet, using the pile of blankets as support. "It would explain everything…" he said softly, his eyes aglow with excitement. "Why the caves are sacred, why the warnings of the Dursturock are so clear, why the prophecies came true…"

"… because it all happened before…"

"Exactly!" The old man smiled, his confidence restored. He beamed at Cara, pride and respect gleaming in his eyes.

Leolin gazed at them both with dismay, crestfallen. "How could you believe that?" he asked incredulously. "The Creator showed us these caves so our ancestors could shelter from the Dursturock. It's so much easier to explain all of this with the Creator. How can you be so blind to the truth?"

Cara snorted. "I could say the same to you. The easiest way out isn't always the correct one."

A noise came from outside of the storage room. Cara heard footsteps shuffling down the carved stone corridor, echoing across the chambers. Within moments they stopped outside of the hole in the wall and a large surly face appeared in the entrance.

"Hello," said Cara cheerfully, too elated to worry about the priest. "Would you like some blankets?"

139

The large priest scowled. "Someone reported seeing the heretic…" he stopped as his eyes fell on Bakinu. "Well I never…" he stepped into the storage room and approached the old man, grabbing him roughly by the arm. "You're not welcome here. I'll escort you out of the caves." Bakinu looked frightened by the man's burly grasp, but he was not strong enough to resist.

"Stop!" yelled Cara. The priest ignored her and led Bakinu to the door. She jumped in front of them and put her hands across the hole. "I said stop!"

The priest frowned at her. "Move out of the way. I have a job to do."

Cara put her hands on her hips. "Do you know who I am?"

The priest eyed her cautiously. "Yes."

"Then you know who I will tell about this incident. This man is under my personal protection, and you may *not* remove him from these caves."

The priest watched her carefully, weighing his options. Finally he shrugged. "Fine. We'll bring him to the High Priest. He'll know what to do." Before Cara could protest he pushed her out of the way with one arm and stepped through the hole, dragging Bakinu behind him with the other. Leolin shot Cara a furtive glance before following. Cara trailed behind, anxiously watching as the old man limped ahead of her.

The older priest led them through several side corridors, avoiding the main cavern chamber. The smooth black walls gleamed from the lantern in Leolin's hands. Small dark holes opened up from the walls into other storage rooms. After a few more turns they emerged into a medium sized chamber, but this one was richly furnished. Thick carpets covered the ground and a large desk and chair sat at the back of the room. Cara was immediately reminded of her father's office at the church. It had the same layout and colors, minus the shiny black obsidian rock lining the ceiling and walls. Her father, as always, was hunched over his desk, contemplating a Penlet laid open before him. Several priests bustled around the room, delivering inventory reports and stockroom numbers. At the sound of the group entering the High Priest looked up from his desk. He frowned at the sight of Bakinu.

"Thank you, Wilhelm," he said to the large priest, his voice strained with fatigue. "You may leave now." He looked around the room. "You may all leave, except Bakinu and my daughter."

The priests scurried to vacate the room, nearly tripping over each other in their haste. When Leolin started to join them, the High Priest called out. "Not you Leolin. I want you to stay right here." Leolin gulped and remained by Cara's side. After the room was empty, Cara's father slowly stood up from his desk and approached the group. He stopped several feet away and gazed at the three of them, his eyes accusing.

"Cara," he barked suddenly. "I told you to stay away from this heretic. You disobeyed me."

Cara flushed red with anger. "I didn't..."

"It was my fault, sir," Leolin interrupted.

The High Priest whirled on him. "You are right, it is. How is it that she can still get into trouble, with you watching her every second?"

Leolin turned a deep red and looked down at his shoes in embarrassment.

"And you," he continued, rounding on Bakinu. "You have brought destruction upon us all. Must you continue your heresy by corrupting my daughter too?"

"It's not his fault!" Cara burst out. "I can think for myself."

The High Priest whirled around and walked to his desk, turning his back on his daughter and resting his hands on the desk's surface. "You leave me no choice, Cara. This man is a danger to you and to this village. He must be removed from these caves."

"If this is your decision, then I will leave," Bakinu said softly.

Cara rounded on him. "Not you, too," she scolded. She turned back to her father. "The caves are a place of safety. The Dursturock cannot harm us in here, no matter who we shelter."

Her father shook his head. "Even so, the people do not want him here. He is a heretic, a blasphemer. They blame this all on him, and rightfully so."

"But…"

"He must go. It is my final decision."

Cara clenched her fists, her eyes narrowed as she stared at her father's back. "Fine. Then I'll go too."

Her father turned around slowly, clenching his jaw. "No, you won't. I won't let you."

"All I have to do is tell them," she said slowly, an idea dawning on her. She swallowed nervously, embracing the idea as it spread through her mind. "As soon as they hear that I'm an atheist, they won't tolerate me being here either. They might even kick you out for hiding me all of these years."

The High Priest stood very still, staring eye to eye with his daughter. A few tense moments passed. Bakinu and Leolin exchanged worried looks. Finally, the High Priest backed down. He whirled around and strode to the other side of his desk, sitting in the large armchair and gazing at the three villagers with contempt.

"Fine," he spat out. "The heretic may stay. Try and keep him away from the other villagers. Now get out of my sight."

Chapter Fourteen

The night passed in a whirl. Blankets were handed out to the villagers and everyone slept on the floor of the main cavern. Although physically and mentally exhausted, Cara had a restless night. The floor was hard, the room was crowded, and there was a certain chill to the air that no blanket could cure. She was relieved when a priest announced the rising of the sun from the cave entrance.

Cara yawned and sat up, still holding the blanket tight around her shoulders. The floor of the cave was coming to life, the villagers slowly stirring and emerging from their blankets. A baby started crying on the other side of the cave. The piercing wails echoed off the high ceiling of the cave, and only stopped when its mother began to feed it.

"Good morning."

Cara looked around and saw Bakinu standing behind her, three bowls of mash in his hands. He held one out to her, and she accepted it readily. She was surprised to see how little there was in the bowl. It was almost half of what she was used to.

"One for you too," Bakinu added, holding out a bowl to Cara's right. She looked over and saw Leolin frowning, still curled up under his blanket. After a few awkward moments he pushed himself up and accepted the bowl, reluctantly mumbling his thanks. Cara slowly took a bite of the grain mash, watching the cave come to life around her. White robed priests navigated the cavern with skill, stepping over small streams of water and sleeping villagers while handing out bowls of mash and cups of water. She grimaced at the watery mixture as it touched her tongue, but her hunger overcame her repulsion. She shoveled down the rest of the bowl quickly. When she finished, she stood up and stretched, looking around curiously.

"Don't go anywhere," Leolin said quietly, still spooning his mash into his mouth.

Cara looked down at him, irritated. "Who said I was going anywhere?"

Leolin took another bite and swallowed deliberately. "We're going to stay right here in the main cavern with everyone else. It's safe and you won't get into trouble."

Cara glared at him for a moment and then sat down abruptly, crossing her arms over her chest. "There's nowhere to go, anyway. What are we supposed to do? We can't just sit here until the Dursturock goes away."

Leolin shrugged. "That's exactly what we'll do, until we're told otherwise. The priests are studying the Penlet right now. They'll know what to do."

Bakinu put down his empty plate and sighed, leaning back on his thin arms. "I don't think anyone knows what to do now, not even the priests."

Leolin glared at him, his calm demeanor cracking under the pressure of the last few days. "No one asked you, baki."

Bakinu stiffened a little at the insult, but remained silent. Cara frowned at Leolin then turned to the old man, baiting Leolin. "The Dursturock's an animal. Maybe we just need to scare it away."

Leolin groaned. "Not this again…"

Bakinu smiled, catching on. "We could throw rocks and yell at it. I'm sure it will go away eventually."

Leolin cleared his throat. "I think that's enough nonsense. The Penlet says that our ancestors sheltered in these caves for 14 years. We must do the same."

"Fourteen years seems like an awful long time to wait," Cara mused. "I'm sure our ancestors got a little confused."

"I bet it will be gone in a month," Bakinu stated confidently, winking at Cara.

"A month!" exclaimed Leolin, turning red in the face. "You wouldn't! To go outside that soon would be certain death!"

"I'd say a week," countered Cara, barely able to contain her smile.

"You…" Leolin stopped, looking suspiciously between the two. "Ah, I see. You're joking about the Dursturock. Cara, this is no laughing matter."

Cara shrugged her shoulders and sighed. "No, I guess not. But I still want to know if we can stop it. Maybe we should go outside and see if it's still there."

"Its magic is too powerful," Bakinu stated. "All it would have to do is roar, and we'd be helpless. There's nothing to do but wait."

"But for how long?"

Before anyone could answer, a soft bell rang from the far corner of the cave. The murmur of voices stopped as a small collection of priests poured out of a nearby corridor. The last one out was the High Priest, resplendent in his golden-trimmed white robes. He strode across the cavern and climbed on top of a short stocky stalagmite, using the glossy black steps that were carved into its side. All eyes were on the High Priest as he righted himself on top of the rock and gazed over his people.

"Praise the Creator," he began.

"We praise the Creator in all His glory," responded the villagers in unison.

The High Priest nodded, satisfied. "Count yourselves blessed on this day. We are alive. The Dursturock has come, and we are still here. Our prayers have been answered."

Everyone nodded vigorously and many made the sign of the Creator, touching their fingertips together and then to their foreheads.

"Despite our good fortunes, there are still hard times ahead." Cara's father paused, his eyes sweeping over the crowd. "Life in these caves will not be easy. There will be challenges. Obstacles. Trials to test our faith."

Cara rolled her eyes and looked over at Bakinu. The old man was staring at the High Priest with a slightly worried expression. Cara snorted. *How can he be taking my father so seriously?*

"Our first test begins today."

Cara looked back at her father, slightly surprised. *Today?*

The High Priest gazed solemnly at his people. "Our food stores will only last until the end of the week."

The cave erupted into noise. A few villagers gasped in concern, some shouted out questions, and others simply stared, too stunned for words. The High Priest raised his hands to regain control, but the room would not fall silent. It took a few minutes of priests circling around and calming individuals before the talking ceased and silence finally fell. The High Priest lowered his hands and cleared his throat.

"I know this seems unfair. But, with the Creator's help, we can make it through these trying times. These caves are much larger than they appear. There are miles of unexplored passages continuing deep under the hills. With any luck there will be a source of food somewhere in those depths. I call on all of you who are able and willing to join the priests in their search. Until we find more food, we will have to ration what is left. Be at peace, and have faith in the Creator. He will give us strength."

The High Priest climbed down from his pedestal and began talking to several senior priests. Everyone in the room started talking again, the worried whispers bouncing around the cavern. A few people stood up and walked to the front, presumably volunteering to help. Cara stared at the collection of priests at the front of the room, a nervous pit forming in her stomach. She had counted on being bored and living in close quarters, but she hadn't even thought about running out of food. *How could this happen? How are we going to find anything edible underground?*

"Are you okay?"

Bakinu's worried voice snapped Cara out of her trance. She smiled. "Yeah, I'm fine. I just didn't think the situation was so desperate."

Bakinu shrugged. "There are a lot of people here. Over two hundred. The food stores couldn't last forever."

Leolin shook his head. "Maybe not, but they should have lasted a lot longer than this. The priests are supposed to keep the grain stores replenished at all times. It says so in the Penlet."

"Well clearly someone messed up," Cara retorted. She stood up and shook out her hair, throwing it up into a ponytail.

Leolin eyed her warily. "What are you doing?"

She ignored him and began walking towards the priests.

"Wait!" She heard Leolin scrambling behind her as he jumped to his feet and rushed after her. "Where are you going?"

"To volunteer," she said calmly, continuing to walk across the cave. She stepped over several people and navigated around a small trickling canal of water.

"I don't think that's a good idea," Leolin answered, catching up with her and walking by her side. "Your father wants me to make sure you don't get into any trouble."

"And my father also asked for anyone able and willing to help. Well, I'm able and I'm willing. It sure beats sitting in this cave all day."

Another person jogged up behind them. Cara turned and saw Bakinu walking behind her. "What?" he said defensively. "You think an old man can't help look for food too?"

Cara smiled. "Sorry, of course you can. I should have asked."

They arrived at the front of the cave. Red and white-robed priests rushed past them, organizing other volunteers and planning out search routes.

"You three together?" A tall thin priest called out from the center of the gaggle. Cara nodded. "Good. I'll put you with

Wilhelm. He's exploring the fourth northwest corridor." The priest turned and cupped his hands around his mouth. "Hey Wilhelm! I've got a group for you!"

A burly thickset man with jet black hair muscled his way through the crowd. His white robe fell like a tent around his large frame, and his face was creased with deep frown lines. Cara shifted uncomfortably. She knew him as one of the more unpleasant priests under her father's command. He was brusque, rude, and generally hard to get along with.

Wilhelm approached them and frowned, staring down at the group. He was very tall, and towered quite easily over Cara. He looked them over quickly, then grunted and started to walk away. When the group didn't follow, he paused and turned around. "Are you coming or not?"

Leolin blushed and started forward quickly, with Cara and Bakinu right behind him. Together they each grabbed a lantern and followed Wilhelm out of the main cavern and into the northwest corridor. The group walked in silence, alone in the long tunnel as it continued deeper into the hills. After a few minutes, they passed three different rocky openings in the walls. At the fourth one, Wilhelm stopped and turned around, holding the lantern high in the air above his head. The light bounced off the walls and highlighted the angles on his face, making him much more imposing than before.

"We go in here," he said abruptly. "If we find a branch we split up into two groups. If it branches again you go alone. Don't spend more than twenty minutes on your own before checking in with your partner. I'll come and get you when I decide we're done. Do you understand?"

Cara shifted uncomfortably. "Yes."

Leolin edged closer to her. "I'll travel with Cara. I'm supposed to look after her."

"No," growled Wilhelm.

Leolin stared at him, slightly taken aback. "Ah, well…I think maybe…"

Wilhelm pointed at Bakinu, an ugly scowl on his face. "I will not go with that heretic. The Creator only knows why he has been allowed to live this long."

Cara stiffened. "I don't…"

Leolin quickly put his hand on her shoulder and talked over her. "Of course, of course, you're right. I'll go with him. I trust you'll take good care of the High Priest's daughter."

Wilhelm simply turned around and strode into the dark opening, his lantern swinging in front of him. Cara made a rude gesture at his back and then followed, with Leolin and Bakinu close behind.

The rocky corridor was dark and dry. Obsidian rock glittered all around, its sharp edges thrusting out into the corridor from odd angles. The passageway twisted back and forth, rising and falling in steep rocky ledges. The smooth polished floor of the main cavern was replaced with abrupt rock faces and sudden drops. As the group continued to travel, the passage widened and narrowed periodically. At one point the walls came so close together that Wilhelm had to stand sideways and shuffle to make it through. Cara found her mind wandering as they hiked. She imagined giant queechees using these caves as a lair, and she pretended that every gleam of the lantern on the walls was a small burst of flame. After more than ten minutes, the passageway finally forked. A large open hole led to the right, and a small narrow passage curved sharply to the left. Wilhelm stopped at the split and turned around.

"You two go to the left. We'll take the right."

"Hang on a second," Cara said, putting her hands on her hips. "Why can't I go with Bakinu?"

Leolin shook his head vigorously. "Absolutely not. He's been a bad enough influence…" his eyes flickered towards Wilhelm, "…I mean, he's dangerous and I don't want you spending time with him."

Bakinu shot her a look, shaking his head subtly from side to side. Cara swallowed her angry retort and frowned. "Fine, whatever. Let's get this over with."

The group split up. Wilhelm led Cara quickly down the right-hand path, moving his bulky frame surprisingly quickly over the rough ground. Cara scrambled to keep up. After only a few minutes the passageway narrowed and forked again. Wilhelm stopped and examined the openings as Cara caught up, panting slightly.

"The right fork is too narrow for me," he said, eyeing it warily. "I'll take the left; you take the right. We meet back here in twenty minutes. Understand?"

"Yes," Cara replied, sullen.

Wilhelm looked at her, his eyes softening for a second. "Be careful," he added, for once recognizing her identity. Before she could reply, he was off, moving briskly down the left passageway.

"Goodbye to you, too," muttered Cara as she headed off to the right. She slipped past the narrow entrance and edged in sideways, holding her lantern out in front of her. For a few minutes, she walked in silence. The ground was particularly rocky here, and she had to stare at her feet to keep her balance. The lantern light played tricks on her eyes, and she almost tripped and fell several times. The passageway stayed quite narrow, only a few feet wide at some parts. Finally, the passage came to a dead end. She stopped and held the lantern up, examining the wall in front of her. The high ceiling arched down and joined the wall, shining black in the lantern light.

"Well that was unexciting," she commented, examining the walls. There were absolutely no signs of life. Just rock, rock, and more rock, like the rest of the caves. Just as she was about to turn around she noticed a dark spot near the ground that the light wasn't illuminating properly. She crouched down and examined it further. To her surprise the light in her lantern started flickering slightly, steadily blowing towards the wall in front of her.

"Huh," she said aloud. "Now what do we have here?"

She leaned forward and looked into the blackness. There was a crack near the ground, about a foot and a half wide and two feet tall. A gentle breeze floated through the hole, sucking the air from the cave in through the narrow opening. Cara stared at the crack for a few moments. It was small, yes, but not too small for her slender frame. Her arms were lanky, but her shoulders were still fairly narrow. She lay down on the ground and scooted a little closer. *Yeah, I can fit. A little tight, but no problem. I'll just have to push the lantern ahead of me.* She stopped and considered it. This probably wasn't a great idea. It would take a while to get in and out, and there might not even be anything at the end of the tunnel. But Wilhelm knew she was here, and there was that breeze…maybe there was life at the other end? She imagined herself walking back, proudly announcing that she had found food and everyone would be okay. She would be the hero, the one who saved everyone from starvation. Surely it was worth the risk? She clenched her teeth, grabbed the lantern and pushed forward, thrusting her body into the crack as darkness consumed her.

Chapter Fifteen

Cara pushed her body further and further into the crack, nudging the lantern ahead of her. The stone closed in all around her, jagged black edges poking into her right side as she shuffled along the ground. The air continued to flow past her, whistling slightly as it lifted her hair and slipped past her eardrums. Cara continued to push herself forward foot by foot, scrunching her body then extending it by pushing off of the floor with her feet. After a few minutes she began to tire. Her arms ached, her legs ached, and she was slightly short of breath. Cara paused briefly and straightened out, looking down past her feet. The passage-way behind was completely dark. The light from the lantern didn't make it far past her toes, and her body was blocking most of it. She took a deep breath and pushed on. After several more tense minutes, the tunnel finally began to widen. Cara was able to shift onto her hands and knees, and soon after she was able to walk at a crouch. She felt herself relaxing as the stone walls dropped away and the space became bigger. Finally, the walls and ceiling leaped away, and she found herself standing in a large empty space. She held up the lantern and looked around.

The space looked a lot like the caves before, except there was a very large pile of rocks in front of her blocking off most of the cave. The rocks looked shattered, as if they had fallen from the ceiling and crashed into this pile of rubble. Cara examined the rocky face. It was at least twelve feet tall, packed solid with large and small obsidian fragments. She held up her lantern a little higher, trying to see the ceiling past the blockage, but the lantern light wasn't strong enough. There was nothing else to do – she had to climb. Cara approached the wall and stepped cautiously on a large black rock. It didn't move. Encouraged, she used her hand and other foot to cautiously move her way up a couple feet higher, dangling the lantern above with her other hand. Halfway up, she took a short break, evaluating the rest of the climb to find the best footholds. As she panted quietly to herself, she thought she heard a slight noise. She took a breath and held it for as long as she could. There, a slight rustle. She let her breath out and resumed climbing, excited to see what was making the noise. Slowly but surely she climbed the rocky face, until finally she reached the top. She held up the lantern and gasped at what she saw.

It was a lake! A massive pool of dark water lay in the center of a large empty cavern. The water was perfectly still, not a ripple or a wave breaking the surface. Large lumps emerged from the water, creating a treacherous maze of sharp obsidian protrusions that stood out like hundreds of tiny islands. Cara stood at the top of the rock face, balanced precariously on a narrow ledge of broken rock. Suddenly she heard another rustle and a plop. A small ripple appeared in the lake. Surprised, Cara leaned too far forward and began to fall. She thrust out her hands and caught a tenuous grip on the wall, barely grasping the rocks with her fingers. She narrowly avoided falling off the ledge, but the lantern wasn't so lucky. It swung out of her grasp and soared down towards the lake, shattering on the rocky dam at the edge of the water below. The tinkling of glass echoed throughout the cave, and then the world was plunged into darkness.

Cara remained frozen, clutching the wall with all her strength. Everything was black. Completely black. She had never experienced such darkness. She blinked several times, trying to see if her eyes were actually open. It was frightening. No, it was terrifying. Was this what it felt like to be blind? At night there were stars, there was the moon, and there were candle lights and fires. But here there was nothing. Just darkness. Everywhere.

Another rustle broke the silence. Cara let loose a breath she didn't realize she was holding. She forced herself to move through the darkness, slowly feeling her way until the ground beneath her felt wide and more firm. She crouched down, too afraid to move any further. Even with light it would be hard to make it to the bottom of this rock pile. Cara didn't even want to think about doing it in darkness. She swallowed, trying to push down a lump of fear that began to rise inside her. *It's funny how you start to appreciate things once you don't have them. Light is such a wonderful thing. I really wish I had a lantern right now.* Cara took a deep breath and closed her eyes.

"They know I'm here," she said aloud, trying to stay calm. "It's probably been at least twenty minutes. Wilhelm will come for me, and then I'll be okay." She opened her eyes. Everything was still black. Impossibly black.

What if they don't come? She rebuked herself. *Of course they'll come. You're the High Priest's daughter. They would never leave you here. All they have to do is...*she paused. The crack – would they see it? Would they know where she went? And more importantly, would they be able to fit? Wilhelm was too large to even enter the passageway. He would never be able to crawl through that crack. It could take a while till they found someone small enough to follow her. *What if they don't make it on time? What if...*

Another rustle broke her train of thought, followed by several quieter sounds. A small plop of water echoed through the cave. Cara turned her head towards the sound, and stared with useless eyes. What was that noise? Was it dangerous? Did it know she was up here? *I can't stay; I've got to get out of here. I've got to take my chances.*

Cara carefully extended an arm and felt below her for a large strong rock. She found one after a minute, and carefully began to shift her weight onto it. Before she could finish, however, the rock shifted. A cracking noise split the air and a torrent of clacking and roaring followed. Cara jumped back to her secure position and waited out the rockslide, trembling with fear as she listened to the rocks slowly come to a stop. There was nothing else to do. She would simply have to wait.

Time seemed to pass very slowly. She thought about trying to take a nap, but the thought of rolling over in her sleep into a pitch black avalanche soon cured her of that. She counted imaginary odenpom jumping over fences, she made up a story about flying on an iraa bird, and she even recited some Penlet passages she had memorized. The time wore on. As she sat in the darkness, unable to see, she focused on her other senses, especially her hearing. The cave was completely quiet, save for the occasional rustling noise. She began to notice a pattern. After almost every rustle there was a small plop, some larger and some so faint you could barely hear them. Sometimes there was a slight slithering noise, as if something was dragging along the ground. The longer she sat there the more she began to wonder. Her fear gradually melted away to curiosity. What could possibly be making that noise? It could be more falling rocks, but the pattern made her think it was probably not inanimate. That would mean it's an animal. But what animal could live down here?

A large rustle echoed through the air. Cara turned her head and listened carefully. That one was different. It continued, growing slightly louder as it slithered. Cara cocked her head to the side. Something was wrong. The sound was coming from a different direction. It was coming from…the entrance?

"Cara?" a dim voice shouted from a distance. "Cara, are you there?"

Cara had to restrain herself from jumping up and cheering. "I'm here!" she shouted back, relief making her voice crack. "I'm here, please help me! I can't see anything – I dropped my lantern!"

The rustling resumed, more frantic than before. "Hang on, I'm coming!" A few minutes passed. Cara started to see a faint glow in the air, coming from the crack in the wall. The glow grew brighter and brighter, until finally a lantern emerged, held by a pale hand.

"I'm here!" she shouted again. Leolin slowly emerged from the crack, his long dark hair a tousled mess over his pale face as he squeezed out from the rock and clambered to his feet. He looked around frantically, holding up the lantern and squinting into the darkness. "Where?"

"Up here, on the rocks!"

Leolin turned and looked up. "What are you doing up there?"

Cara shrugged. "I wanted to see what was on the other side. I found a lake."

"Okay, I'm climbing up now."

"Be careful," Cara warned. "The rocks are unstable."

Leolin began to climb, slowly maneuvering his way through the large shards of obsidian. As he came closer, the light began to hurt Cara's eyes. She looked away towards the lake, blinking from the bright light. The darkness of the lake began to melt away slightly as the lantern light spilled over the rocky dam. She blinked several times, trying to focus on the lake. To her surprise she saw movement. A furry figure darted across the shore and jumped into the lake with a plop. After a few moments it emerged onto a small obsidian island and crawled out of sight, its wet tail slithering on the rocks. Dozens of other forms darted across the rocks, some only a few feet away at the bottom of the ledge. Something about the way they moved seemed familiar. Almost like…

"Dunbee!" Cara shouted suddenly. "Leolin, I see dunbee!"

Leolin paused and looked up, confused, almost at the top. "What?"

Cara turned back to him, her eyes bright with excitement. "There's life here! Dunbee, I'm sure of it! I've been hearing all sort of noises, and it's the dunbee! A lot of them too."

Leolin finally reached Cara, stepping precariously onto the ledge near the wall. He put a hand on Cara's shoulder and examined her closely. "Are you okay? Did you get hurt at all?"

Cara shrugged him off. "I'm fine. We need to catch some of those dunbee!"

Leolin shook his head. "Absolutely not. We're going back to the main cave. We can tell the priests about this place, and they can worry about catching dunbee." He turned and looked back down the slope. "This is going to be tricky. You go first, and I'll follow with the lantern."

Cara thought about arguing, but Leolin made sense. There was no reason to get them now, and she was eager to leave this place. She nodded and began climbing down, using the lantern light to guide her path. After a few tense minutes she and Leolin made it to the ground. Leolin sighed with relief, and Cara leaned against the wall, exhausted.

"How long has it been?" she asked, glancing at Leolin.

Leolin combed a hand through his dark hair. "Almost an hour. Wilhelm was beside himself. He tried to come in after you, but he was too large for the passageway. When he told us we were terrified. Lucky for you I'm pretty skinny." He grinned awkwardly, clearly relieved that his plan had worked.

"Thanks," Cara murmured. "I was starting to get a little scared."

"A little?" scoffed Leolin. "I would be terrified!"

They both took a deep breath and entered the crack in the wall, Leolin leading with the lantern. It was a tight fit for Leolin, but with a lot of effort he made it through. They navigated their way back down the narrow passageway and traveled for several minutes in silence, quickly scurrying over rocky protuberances and outcroppings. Finally they squeezed through the final corridor, and Cara heard Bakinu shout with glee. He rushed to her and hugged her tightly, his thin arms surprisingly strong for an old man.

"Hey, I'm okay," she said, a little flustered.

Bakinu withdrew, giving her a scolding glare. "Don't you ever do that to me again. I thought you were dead! Fallen down a hole, or lost forever!"

Wilhelm scowled at her, angry at her for disappearing but clearly relieved to see her alive and well. "Why did you not return?"

"I dropped my lantern, and I couldn't get down from the ledge I was on," she explained, staring at him steadily. "But I found life. There's a lake, with dozens of Dunbee!"

Wilhelm squinted. "Dunbee? In these caves?"

Cara nodded. "I'm sure of it."

Bakinu smiled. "That must be where the missing grain went."

"Ah, of course!" exclaimed Leolin. "Dunbee have poor eyesight. The lack of light wouldn't bother them at all. It would be easy for them to navigate that corridor to reach the food. The grain stores never stood a chance."

Wilhelm grunted. "We need to get back, report what we've found. Follow me." He turned and set off back down the passageway, his lantern swinging in his hand. Cara followed Leolin very closely, using his lantern light to navigate the rocky floor. Bakinu followed close behind her, providing additional light to walk by. Cara felt grateful for their presence. She thought back to the darkness before, and shivered at the memory. At least she was safe now. With friends. She smiled at the term. Yes, that's what she would call them. They were her friends. Weird, wacky friends, one of which was old enough to be her grandfather and another who annoyed as much as amused her. But friends nonetheless. It had been so long since she'd used the word. No one in school dared to spend too much time with her. And they would certainly never crawl through a crack in a wall to find her.

The group emerged from the final passageway into the northwest corridor. To Cara's relief the floor transitioned to smoother polished rock, the careful work of centuries of diligent priests. Wilhelm turned left and headed towards the main cavern, walking quickly with his large white robes swirling around his feet. As they grew closer to the main cave Cara began to hear shouts up ahead. There was some sort of a commotion going on – a big one, by the sound of it. Leolin looked back and exchanged worried looks with Cara and Bakinu. Wilhelm ignored them and continued on, speeding up his pace. The shouts up ahead grew louder.

Finally they emerged into the main cavern. The place was abuzz with activity. Most of the villagers were pressed up against the cavern walls, leaving the center of the cave empty. A few priests ran around the middle of the giant circle, waving their lanterns above their heads frantically and dashing randomly behind large carved pedestals of obsidian. Shouting rang out from the crowd, and one woman screamed in fright.

"What's going on?" asked Cara, examining the scene.

"I don't know," murmured Leolin, just as confused as Cara. "What are they looking at?"

Wilhelm lifted his arm and pointed up at the ceiling, his finger thick and stubby. Cara followed his gaze. A small form flapped frantically overhead, periodically dive bombing the priests below. An angry screech echoed off the wall, coming from the small creature as it flew across the cave. One villager threw a spoon at it, but it nimbly flipped over in midair and dodged the object.

"What in the Creator's name is that thing?" Leolin exclaimed. It was hard to tell in the dark. The lantern light did not extend to the top of the cave, and the creature was shadowed in darkness. Only when it dived down to attack a priest below did the light highlight its features. Cara got a better look when it dive-bombed closer to the group. The winged form was covered in small, soft scales, glittering green in the lantern light. A long tail was balanced on the other end by a long flexible neck, and at the end rested a thin tapered head with a fierce expression. Black pupils narrowed between golden irises, as the jaws of the queechee opened up and a familiar battle cry rang out.

Chapter Sixteen

"Cheea!" the old man exclaimed. The queechee pulled up hard and angled around at the sound of Bakinu's voice, swerving around the frightened priest below as he dove to the ground and pulled his hands above his head for protection. Cheea whipped her head around and looked in the old man's direction. She screeched again, her voice now filled with happiness and excitement instead of anger.

"Cheea" Bakinu shouted again, stepping forward with his arms raised. Cheea flapped towards him and landed on his arm gracefully, trilling in satisfaction as she settled on his shoulder and rubbed her scaly head across his cheek.

A priest rushed forward, brandishing a long stick and a lantern. "Get it!" shouted voices from the crowd.

"No!" yelled Cara.

Cheea opened her mouth at the priest, trying to give a warning shot, but no flame came out. Cara jumped between the priest and Cheea and threw out her arms. "Stop!"

The priest came to an abrupt stop, startled to see the High Priest's daughter in front of him. Everyone fell silent, watching the situation with apprehension. After a few tense moments a figure emerged from the crowd. The High Priest strode forward and stopped a few feet from Bakinu, glaring at the old man and the queechee.

"What is this creature doing here?" he growled. The cave was completely silent. Only the trickling of the stream broke the silence.

Bakinu trembled slightly. "I think...I mean..." he swallowed and tried again. "She's my pet."

"Your pet?" the High Priest exclaimed. "Queechees are not pets. That animal is a danger to everyone in this cave. Remove it immediately."

Bakinu flinched. "Please...please, sir. She won't hurt anyone now, I promise. She's like family..."

"Now," growled the High Priest. White robes began closing in around Bakinu, hesitantly reaching for the queechee. Cheea hissed and opened her jaw wide, baring her sharp white teeth.

"STOP," countered Cara, planting herself squarely in front of Cheea. "You can't take her." The priests stopped and gazed at her, unsure.

The High Priest glowered at his daughter. "Cara, step aside. This does not concern you."

She crossed her arms and glared back. "I think it does. Remember our deal, father."

The High Priest stood as still as the rocks around him, his gaze as cold as ice. Father and daughter stared resiliently at each other, both refusing to blink. No one dared to breathe. After a few moments the High Priest glowered and gave in. "Fine. The animal stays. Make sure it stays out of my sight."

Murmurs swept across the crowd.

"What?" exclaimed a deep, gravelly voice. Wilhelm stepped forward from the crowd and pointed at the old man and his pet. "We already must live with this heretic among us. Must we also live with his demon pet too?"

The High Priest whirled on his servant, his face contorted with anger. "Are you challenging my authority?"

The large priest cowered at the venom in his voice. "No," he added quietly, the fight gone out of him.

"Good," the High Priest said tersely. He spun around and strode out of the cavern, disappearing into one of the corridors. The crowd slowly began to disperse, many shooting furtive looks at Bakinu, Cara, and Cheea. Within minutes they were alone in a corner of the cavern, a wide ring of space left between them and the nearest family. Leolin hung awkwardly near Cara, reluctant to be associated with Bakinu but unwilling to leave Cara alone with him. Cheea began purring contentedly, rubbing her side against Bakinu's shoulder. Bakinu absently stroked her delicate head, still in shock from the encounter with the High Priest.

Cara turned to him and grinned. "We did it!" she exclaimed. "I can't believe Cheea found us!"

Bakinu blinked. "I never thought…" his voice cracked slightly and he paused, looking at Cheea fondly and lifting her chin with a finger. "I never thought I'd see her again." Cara reached over and stroked Cheea's spine. The queechee trilled in pleasure, arching her back and closing her eyes.

"You're pushing your luck, Cara," Leolin said, eyeing the queechee nervously. "It's only a matter of time before that animal hurts someone."

Cara frowned. "Cheea wouldn't hurt someone unless they tried to hurt her."

Leolin shook his head. "Even the Creator did not extend His mercy over the queechees. They're vicious animals, and they're not to be trusted."

"That's not true," Bakinu stated quietly. "Cheea is the most loyal friend I've ever had."

"They're dangerous!" countered Leolin. "Do you know how many houses and crops they have burned over the years? They even burned down the church once, several generations ago."

"Cheea didn't burn anyone," replied Bakinu. "She didn't even use her fire, even when you were threatening her."

The image of Cheea's angry open mouth swam before Cara's eyes. *That isn't right. Why didn't she use her fire…it looked like she was trying to…*

"That doesn't mean she won't in the future," Leolin responded, slightly louder. "Your emotional attachment to that animal…"

"She's not just an animal," Bakinu interrupted, turning slightly red in the face. "She's much more…"

"Hang on," Cara said loudly, bringing the fight to a standstill. "Something's not right." She ran her hand through her hair, thinking hard. "Cheea tried to use her fire when that priest came at her with the stick. I saw her. She opened her mouth and breathed, but nothing came out."

Bakinu and Leolin stared at her for a moment. "So?" Leolin asked.

Cara looked at Bakinu. "Tell her to breathe fire."

The old man blinked. "Why?"

"Just do it."

Bakinu raised his hand in the air and made a fist. Cheea watched it with keen eyes, straightening her neck and ceasing her purring. After a moment he opened the fist, quickly flicking his fingers out until his hand was splayed wide open. Cheea opened her mouth and exhaled, her belly contorting with the effort. Leolin squeaked and ducked, diving to the ground to avoid the hot blast. Nothing happened. No flame, no heat, nothing. Leolin looked up from the ground, frowning. Bakinu made the gesture again, and Cheea tried to breathe fire again. Nothing came out. Not even a puff of smoke.

"What's the matter Cheea?" Bakinu asked, lifting her chin and looking at her with some concern. Cheea chirped and quivered her body, as if to say she didn't know.

"Why didn't she breathe fire?" Leolin asked, slowly picking himself up off the ground and straightening his robes.

"That's not the right question," Cara said slowly, the pieces falling into place in her head. "We should be asking why can't she breathe fire. Why her powers don't work."

Bakinu turned to her, a puzzled expression on his face. "What do you mean?"

Cara turned to Leolin. "When we were in the cave with the dunbee, did you notice anything strange?"

"Um, not really. I was focused on getting you out of there."

"But the dunbee," Cara persisted. "There were a lot of them..."

Leolin frowned, the puzzle dawning on him. "So...how could we move normally?"

"Exactly," Cara announced. "Time should have slowed down. Something was stopping their magic. Just like with Cheea."

They stood in silence for a moment, pondering the dilemma.

"What does it mean?" Bakinu asked tentatively.

Leolin shrugged. "Only the Creator knows. Truthfully it doesn't matter. It doesn't change anything."

Cara snorted. "How could you say that? Of course it matters!"

"There's probably just something wrong with the queechee. As for the dunbee, who knows. Maybe you weren't close enough to them."

Cara began to pace back and forth, thinking hard. "The Dursturock is an animal. We know it uses a magic roar to scare people."

"Not this again," Leolin groaned.

"Which means," Cara continued, "that the Dursturock's magic doesn't work in these caves either. That's why these caves are safe – the Dursturock can't use its magic in here!"

"The caves are safe because the Creator..."

Cara continued to talk over him. "If there's a way to stop magic, then we can fight back against the Dursturock. Without its roar it's just another animal. And animals can be killed."

"The Dursturock isn't an animal," Leolin argued. "It's the Creator's wrath!"

"What do you think could be blocking the powers?" asked Bakinu, ignoring him.

"I'm not sure," Cara murmured. "Something in the air? The water? Something in the cave?"

"It's probably not food or water. Cheea hasn't had a chance to eat or drink anything."

"Then something in the air?"

"Maybe. But the air is flowing in and out of the cave all the time. Why would the magic only stop in here?"

"So the rocks then?"

"Perhaps. There's no way to know for sure."

Cara looked around nervously. "There's one way to find out. We have to leave the caves."

"NO!" Leolin suddenly shouted. Cara jumped in surprise, startled by the anger in his voice. He glared at Bakinu and Cara, his normally smooth face creased with anger. "You will stop this foolish conversation this instant. You will NOT leave this cave. You will stay here with everyone else and forget all these blasphemous thoughts. Nothing good can come of it."

Cara watched Leolin cautiously. His dark hair was askew, strands falling haphazardly in front of dark eyes which stared directly at Cara. He was furious; there was no doubt about it. He wasn't going to budge. She carefully kept her face neutral and shrugged. "Maybe you're right. It is all a bunch of guess-work anyway. It's probably safer to just stay put."

Bakinu looked at her in surprise. Cara stared at the ground, trying to remain submissive. This would only work if Leolin believed she was sincere.

Leolin narrowed his eyes as he studied her, suspicious. "Well, I'm glad you've found some sense," he said cautiously. "There's nothing we can do right now. Wilhelm is probably reporting the dunbee sighting to the other priests. We'll just wait right here until we're needed."

Cara nodded in agreement and quietly sat down. Bakinu gave her a strange look, but settled down next to her, following suit. Cheea jumped down from his shoulder and curled up in his lap, quickly becoming a tight green ball of scales and wings. Leolin sighed in relief and joined them on the floor, leaning against the wall of the cave with a tired grunt. He dusted off his long red robes, pushed his black hair out of his eyes and closed them, relaxing. Cara also lay down and pretended to nap, listening closely to see if Leolin moved. Several minutes passed. Cara began to notice other sounds in the cave. There were excited voices coming from the far corner of the cave. Cara opened her eyes and saw Wilhelm discussing something with several other priests, including the High Priest. They seemed very excited at his words. Numerous priests disappeared for several minutes, then returned with several apprentice priests, all clutching empty bags. The discussion continued for several minutes until finally one priest left the group and came walking in Cara's direction. She closed her eyes and pretended to be asleep. The footsteps grew closer and then stopped fairly nearby. Cara breathed in and out slowly, trying to imitate the rhythmic breathing of sleep.

"Leolin," a voice said from above, "I need you to come with me."

"I can't," Leolin replied, his voice tired. "I'm supposed to look after Cara."

"New orders," the voice replied. "We're instructed to catch as many dunbee as possible for food, but most of us can't fit through the crack. You're one of the few who can."

"But Cara…"

"I can look after her," the voice said. "She's asleep, anyway. She can't get into much trouble."

Cara could imagine the conflicted expression on Leolin's face. She had to fight to keep the smirk off of her hers.

"Fine. Keep a close eye on her. I'll be back as soon as I can."

Cara listened as one set of footsteps walked away briskly. The other pair stood there for a few minutes. Cara kept her eyes closed and continued to breathe slowly. *Please just go away* she thought fervently.

"I can watch her, sir." Bakinu's voice was timid but steady.

She heard the priest's weight shift. "I don't need advice from you, heretic."

"Of course," Bakinu added hastily. "You have much more important things to do."

"That's an understatement," growled the priest.

Bakinu remained silent, waiting out the priest's impatience.

Several tense minutes passed. Cara could hear the priest's foot tapping in boredom. Finally he cracked. "I suppose you could watch her for a bit. Just while I check in with the other priests."

"Naturally," Bakinu said meekly, the perfect model of sub-missiveness. The priest grunted and then strode off, his heavy footsteps echoing as they faded away in the distance. Cara waited another minute, then cautiously opened one eye. Bakinu sat in front of her, examining her closely. He grinned when he saw her eye open.

"Thanks," Cara whispered. "Is the coast clear?"

"As clear as it's going to get," replied Bakinu. "What's your plan?"

Cara stood up and grabbed a large piece of obsidian from the floor, a wide grin stretching across her face. "Now we go outside."

Chapter Seventeen

Cara and Bakinu strolled casually along the perimeter of the cave, trying to look inconspicuous. Cheea rode silently on Bakinu's shoulder, golden eyes shimmering in the lantern light from the sconces carved into the walls. A few villagers glanced at them, but they looked away quickly when they saw who it was. The part of the cave close to the exit was mostly deserted. Families gave the area a wide berth, as if afraid that the Dursturock would come rushing in at any moment. When they grew close to the entrance, Cara paused and leaned against the wall casually, as if just taking a stroll around the cave. Several villagers were still looking at them, and Cara didn't want them to raise an alarm.

"What if the Dursturock comes?" whispered Bakinu, fear creeping into his voice.

"If it's an animal, like we think, then the chances are slim that it would be there right as we come out," Cara whispered back, "but that's why I brought this." She held up the large chunk of obsidian and showed it to Bakinu. "If there's something about the rock that blocks magic, then this should keep us safe."

"That's a big if," Bakinu said.

Cara shrugged. "Maybe. But it makes sense. What else could be blocking the magic? It's worth a try. We won't be out there for very long anyway. And if it works…" she paused, her eyes shifting to look Bakinu straight on. "The Dunbee won't feed all of us for very long. Either we get rid of the Dursturock, or we start dying."

Bakinu went silent, contemplating her words. After a while the villagers turned their backs, ignoring the odd couple near the wall. Cara silently pushed off from the wall and darted towards the entrance, ducking down and rushing through the low passageway. The corridor grew dark – the lantern light couldn't penetrate past the first few feet, and Cara didn't dare bring a light lest it give away their plan. She slowed down and began to feel her way down the smooth walls. She could hear Bakinu's quiet footsteps following as they shuffled down the path. After a minute she began to see sunlight up ahead. The light grew brighter and brighter until she reached the hanging curtain of grass. She ducked and pushed it aside, and then stepped into the sunlight.

The light was painful to Cara's eyes. It was blindingly bright, a shocking reminder of the darkness of the caves behind them. Cara squinted and held her hand up above her eyes, shielding them from the glare. It was warm out – much warmer than the cool air of the caves. Gentle tendrils of heat snaked across her skin, penetrating her flesh and warming her to the core. A slight breeze passed by, bringing smells of fresh grass and flowers. Cara sighed. Compared to the cool stale air of the caves, this was heaven. Cheea trilled. Cara opened her eyes and looked over at the old man. His chin was tilted up to the sun, eyes closed with a wide smile on his face. Even Cheea was excited. She cooed and pivoted in a little circle on Bakinu's shoulder, glad to have an open sky above again.

"We should get started," Cara said reluctantly. She looked around at the peaceful meadows and hills. There was no sign of the Dusturock, or any other animal for that matter. Just swaying fields of grass. "I don't see anything yet, but it's not safe out here."

"Yes, of course," Bakinu replied. He opened his eyes and looked at Cara. "Lead the way."

Cara set off to the right, walking in a steady line away from the caves. The hills sloped gently down in front of her, leading to the center of the valley. She could make out some of the fields of grain a few miles off, but the church and most of the buildings were blocked by another hill. After a minute she stopped and looked back. They were a fair distance from the caves, but close enough to sprint to safety if the Dursturock should appear.

"Right," she said. "This should be far enough. See if Cheea can breathe fire."

Bakinu stopped next to her and held up his fist. He opened it quickly, and Cheea dropped her jaw and breathed. Nothing came out.

"Okay," Cara said. "Now wait here." She readjusted the heavy rock in her hand and continued to walk down the hill, putting more distance between her and the cave entrance. After another minute, she turned around and stopped. There was now an equal amount of distance between her and Bakinu as there was between Bakinu and the cave.

"Try it now!" she shouted, hoping he could hear her. Cheea was just a small lump of green on his shoulder. Bakinu held up his fist again, and Cheea opened her mouth. A long bright trail of flame shot into the sky. Bakinu's hoot was clearly audible.

"Yeah!" shouted Cara. She ran a little closer, excited. "Try it now!"

Cheea breathed another blast of fire. Cara ran even closer. She continued to narrow the distance bit by bit, and Cheea continued to use her powers. Finally Cara stood just under forty feet away. Bakinu gave the signal, and Cheea let loose another bout of fire. But this time the flame seemed to have trouble. It wavered uncertainly in the air and only went about half as far as the previous flame.

"Did you see that?" Bakinu said, excitedly. "It changed!"

Cara came forward a few more feet, holding up the heavy obsidian rock fragment. "Try it again."

Cheea drew herself up and tried another blast. The flame only extended a foot before sizzling out completely. Cara narrowed the distance to twenty feet, still clutching the large chunk of obsidian in her arms. When Cheea opened her mouth, nothing came out. The fire was gone.

Bakinu looked at Cara with wonder. "You were right…" he said, his voice filled with admiration. "It's something about the rocks….it blocks magic!"

Cara grinned, triumphant. "And now we know its range. If we carry a piece of obsidian with us, we should be immune to the Dursturock!"

"To its roar," Bakinu said wryly, "but not to its teeth."

Cara nodded. "True. We don't even know what it looks like. It must be massive. It tore apart the odenpom like they were nothing."

"CARA!!"

The furious voice split the air with a crack and made Cara jump. She turned around and saw a figure racing towards her. The red robes and dark hair made her heart sink. How did Leolin find her so quickly?

"This won't be pleasant," murmured Bakinu. Cara nodded glumly, watching as Leolin approached, his face flushed red from anger and almost matching the color of his robes.

"What are you doing?" he yelled, coming to a stop near them. He grabbed Cara's arm and pulled her towards the cave. "We need to get back. NOW!"

Cara let herself be pulled towards the cave. "Fine, fine, okay. You don't have to yell."

"Apparently I do!" he shouted, still pulling her. "You just don't listen, do you? The Dursturock is out here! We could die!"

A bright flash of light suddenly bleached out the air all around them. A peal of thunder crashed through the air right after the lightning, causing the ground to shake around them. Cara yelped and tripped over her feet, landing face first in the long grass beneath her.

"RUN!" Leolin yelled. Bakinu pulled her to her feet and they started to run, Cheea clutching onto his shoulder in fright. The group sprinted towards the cave, panting loudly with hearts pounding as they raced towards the entrance. Cara nearly fell again when another flash lit the air, coinciding with a crash of thunder.

"HURRY!" screeched Leolin. Cara continued running. She was a few steps behind them both. The cave entrance was close. Just a little more…

"TTTTHHHHHHUUUUUURRROOOOOAAAAAAW
WWWWWWRRRRRR!"

The roar ripped through the air, echoing across the hills. Cara gasped and fell, losing her balance. This was it. This was the end. *How could I have been so stupid. This was far too dangerous…* she scrambled to her feet and ran for the entrance. She was dimly aware of a thudding from behind. *I can still hear,* she thought frantically. *I can still think…* she looked down at her arms. They were still clutched around the large hunk of obsidian.

"HURRY, CARA, HURRY!" Leolin and Bakinu were at the cave entrance, watching with eyes as wide as belknay eggs. Cara made it to the entrance. Leolin and Bakinu dove into the passageway, but Cara stopped just under the ledge and turned around.

The Dursturock was running up the hill, catching up at a frightening pace. Rippling muscles flexed under black leathery skin, a hulking mass of terror almost eight feet tall and fifteen feet long. Sharp jagged teeth hung from an open salivating mouth at the end of a short thick neck, large yellow eyes gleaming from the front of its head. Cara nearly dropped the rock she was carrying, her eyes widening in terror. Well over a ton of fierce hungry muscle lunged towards the cave entrance, with four powerful legs propelling the beast forward. Cara screamed and dove into the passageway, scrambling to get away from the Dursturock. The beast reached the entrance and jammed its thick head into the passageway. Cara edged backwards, just out of reach of its long teeth. The animal growled, a low deep throbbing that nearly stopped Cara's heart. Long thick claws scraped at the entrance to no avail, the entrance was simply too small for the beast. A few moments passed, measured by Cara's racing heartbeat and the warm rancid odor blowing past her as it breathed into the narrow corridor. Realizing it was defeated, the Dursturock withdrew its head and disappeared from sight.

Hands grasped at Cara from behind and pulled her farther into the passageway. Her legs trembled and gave out from underneath her. She leaned against the wall of the corridor and closed her eyes, trying to regain some self-control. She heard similar thunks to her left and right. She opened her eyes. Leolin and Bakinu had joined her on the floor. Both were completely pale, blood drained from their faces as they trembled in fright. Even Cheea quivered in fear. She snuggled close to Bakinu, tucked under his arm with her head flat against his chest.

"The Dursturock," Leolin said quietly, his voice still breathless from the sprinting. "It's…an animal…"

Laughter bubbled up from deep inside Cara. It spilled out of her lips and consumed her body as she lapsed into a nervous fit of giggles. Bakinu joined in, a jittery tee hee hee that echoed of relief. Even Leolin smiled.

"We made it," Cara finally choked out, between laughs. "We're alive. Did you see that thing? It was massive!"

Bakinu slowly stopped laughing, the nervous energy of a near death experience finally draining away. "The stone worked, Cara. The roar didn't affect our memory. We were not petrified."

"Speak for yourself," Leolin said. "I was scared out of my mind."

"We were all scared," Cara added, "but not out of our minds. We remember what happened. We were in control of our bodies this time."

Leolin leaned his head against the wall. "Why didn't its powers work on us?"

Cara picked the stone off of the floor and handed it to him. "I took this out there with me when we were testing Cheea's powers. The obsidian somehow blocks magic. Cheea couldn't breathe fire when it was near her, and clearly it saved us from the Dursturock's roar."

Leolin held the rock cautiously. He then looked at the walls around him, eyes narrowed. "The entire cave is made of obsidian. No wonder we're protected from the Dursturock's powers."

"Thank goodness the entrance is small," added Bakinu. "Obsidian or not, that beast would have no trouble killing us all if it could get in here."

They fell silent for a few moments, remembering the Dursturock and its massive size and power. Cara shuddered at the memory. How could they possibly hope to stop a creature that large?

"What were you thinking, going out there on your own?" Leolin asked, a trace of the old anger back in his voice.

"I wasn't alone, I had Bakinu," Cara responded. "And anyway, I had to find out what stopped the magic. Now we know."

"It wasn't worth it," Leolin said stubbornly. "You could have been killed."

"I knew you'd say that," Cara snapped back. "That's why I pretended to sleep."

"Hey," Bakinu interrupted. "There's no use arguing about it now. What's done is done. We need to get back to the main cave. I'm sure someone heard that roar, and your father is bound to realize that you're missing by now."

Cara groaned. "Just my luck. This is going to get ugly."

Leolin slowly stood up and extended a hand to Cara and Bakinu. "This time you have something to show for your troubles," he said, pulling them up. "I saw the Dursturock too. Now that we know it's a beast, there might be something we can do to fight it."

Cara gazed at Leolin in surprise. "Wow, Leolin. I didn't think you'd be so easy to convert."

Leolin snorted. "I haven't converted into anything. The Creator made the Dursturock just as before, except now I know he made the Dursturock as a powerful animal with magical abilities. Nothing has changed, except for our ability to fight back."

Cara snorted. "Of course. Then answer me this. Why doesn't the Penlet ever mention the Dursturock as an animal? Don't you think that would be a mighty useful thing for the Creator to tell us?"

Leolin shrugged. "I don't claim to know the Creator's mind. If he didn't tell us then I'm sure there was good reason for it. Or perhaps older generations neglected to transcribe the Penlet accurately."

Cara rolled her eyes and passed him, leading the way back to the main cavern. After a few minutes of walking in the dark and feeling her way through the smooth tunnel, she began to see the soft glow of lantern light ahead.

"Almost there," she called back to the group.

"Do you think they know we were out there?" asked Bakinu.

"Maybe we can sneak back in," said Cara. "If we can just come in unnoticed..." She stepped into the main cavern and trailed off. The entire village was formed in a semi-circle around the entrance of the cave, many bent over in fervent prayer. Every eye in the chamber was locked on her.

"Or not..." she whispered.

Chapter Eighteen

Over a hundred frightened eyes gazed at Cara and her friends. She stared back, startled by their presence. What were they all doing here? How did they know she was...*oh right. The roar.*

"Cara?" a voice called, cracking in disbelief. Cara looked over to see her father standing in the center of the crowd, his hands still clasped together in prayer. She smiled awkwardly. The High Priest dropped his arms and drew himself to his full height, recovering from his shock. He stepped forward out of the crowd, his gilded white robe gleaming in the light from the torches. All eyes followed him as he stopped in front of his daughter, glaring down at her with cool blue eyes.

"Explain yourself," he said, his voice dangerously quiet.

Cara swallowed, her heart fluttering. "I, um..." she paused and swallowed. "I wanted to see if the Dursturock was out there." She drew herself up a little straighter. "And I saw it, father. The Dursturock is an animal! An enormous black beast with giant teeth and huge muscles!"

The High Priest stared at her, his face as hard as the black rocks all around them.

Cara took a deep breath, unnerved by his silence, then continued. "I also wanted to see if the Dursturock's magic was

185

blocked by the rocks in the cave. And it was! The roar had no effect on us, father; we remember everything!"

Her father's eyes flickered to Bakinu and Leolin, acknowledging them for the first time. She could feel them quivering at the wrath in her father's eyes.

"She's right, sir," Leolin said tentatively, his voice thin and wavering. "I saw the beast too. Its powers were blocked by the obsidian."

The High Priest turned his head towards Leolin. "You are relieved," he said quietly, his voice deceptively calm.

There was a long pause. "What?" Leolin said slowly, a confused expression on his face.

"You are finished. Dismissed. Fired. You are no longer an apprentice priest. Get out of my sight."

Leolin's face turned white. He swayed slightly on his feet, his mouth open slightly, gaping in surprise.

"Father…" Cara began.

"Stop," he barked. "This fool has failed at his duty, put you in mortal danger, and is now lying for you. He is worthless."

"But…"

"Please, sir," Bakinu spoke up, trembling slightly in fear. "It was my idea. Please don't blame Cara or Leolin. I encouraged her to go outside."

The High Priest whirled on him, suddenly enraged. He stopped just in front of Bakinu, nose to nose with the old man, eyes narrowed as he breathed shallowly.

"If my daughter wasn't so fond of you," he whispered. "I would kill you where you stand."

Bakinu turned as white as Leolin, but he held his ground. Even Cheea remained silent for once, still perched on the old man's shoulder.

"Father!" Cara yelled. "Stop it! Our deal…"

"Our deal," the High Priest interrupted, "has been changed. You will do what I say, or I will throw this blasphemer to the Dursturock."

"You wouldn't…"

"Priests!" the High Priest shouted. Several burly priests stepped forward from the crowd and grabbed Bakinu by the arms. Cheea screeched and flapped her wings, but Bakinu whispered something to her that calmed her.

"No, father, don't! I'll tell!"

"Go ahead," her father said, facing her. "Tell, and your friend dies."

Cara froze. Her eyes swept over the crowd. So many eyes, all waiting for her to say something. She opened her mouth, but nothing came out. She looked back at Bakinu. His eyes were huge, blue irises contrasting sharply with the stark white skin around them. She looked at her father, desperate. His eyes were glaciers. There was no sympathy or kindness. *He'd do it. He'd really kill Bakinu…*She closed her mouth and looked down at the floor, defeated.

The High Priest turned to his men. "Throw the heretic in one of the storage rooms. Keep him there until I say otherwise. Cara, follow me." His white robe swirled around his legs as he walked away. The crowd quickly parted for him. Cara watched helplessly as the priests roughly escorted Bakinu past the onlookers and into a far corridor. She glanced at Leolin. He stood completely still, his gaze unfocused as he stared at the far wall the cave. He seemed completely unaware of Cara's presence.

"Cara!" Her father's voice cracked like a whip through the air.

"I'm sorry," she whispered before following her father, leaving Leolin behind. Villagers parted in front of her, allowing her to pass easily through the large crowd. Everyone avoided her gaze, as if they were afraid her touch would incur the High Priest's wrath. *They're right,* she though miserably. *It's all my fault. Everyone I touch gets hurt.*

Her father led her to his chambers. The room was completely empty. All of the priests were still in the main cavern. The High Priest sat down at his desk and stared expectantly at his daughter. After a few moments, she slowly took a seat on the other side of the desk, sitting nervously in the large wooden chair. They sat in silence for a minute. Her father watched her closely, eyes narrowed over steepled fingers as he stared at his daughter.

"Father," Cara began hesitantly. "You have to believe me."

"Oh, do I?" he answered, raising an eyebrow.

"The Dursturock is an animal," she continued. "I saw it. I wasn't lying."

"Sometimes," her father said softly, "I can't help but wonder if you are truly my daughter."

Cara felt like someone had punched her in the face. She blinked back tears, stunned.

The High Priest sighed. "You have your mother's stubbornness. It does not suit you."

"Well at least I have her intelligence," Cara snapped back. "Because clearly I didn't get that from you."

Her father gazed at her seriously, unfazed. "What you did was inexcusable. The Dursturock is here. Going outside is not only suicide, it's heresy."

"I'm not lying," Cara hissed. "The Dursturock's an animal. I saw it."

"Even if I believed you," her father said, leaning forward across the desk, "it changes nothing. The Penlet says we must wait for the Dursturock to pass, so that is what we must do."

"Then we'll die!" Cara yelled. "You said it yourself – we only have enough food to last till the end of the week."

"The dunbee you found have extended that time considerably," her father answered calmly.

"Not fourteen years," Cara countered.

"We will find other food sources."

"Really?" Cara laughed. "In these caves? The only reason the dunbee survived was because of the grain stores. If we stay in these caves, then you are condemning us to die."

"And what do you suggest?"

"We fight!" Cara shouted. "The Dursturock is an animal. And animals can be killed. All we need is a weapon and some obsidian, and we can be free from the Dursturock forever."

"Your delusions," her father answered, "are a danger not only to yourself, but to my people. If you try to leave the caves again, I will kill Bakinu. If you try to convince people to join you, I will kill Bakinu. If you misbehave in any way, I will kill Bakinu. Do you understand me?"

Cara trembled in her seat, barely able to contain her rage. She wanted to scream and curse, to throw things at her father's calm face and break him out of his ignorance. *How can he be so blind to the truth? How can he be doing this to me?* Several tense moments passed. The High Priest continued to stare at her. Finally, she nodded, a tiny jerk of her chin to acknowledge his words.

"Good," her father said. "You may leave now. Remember my words – I mean them."

Cara stood up abruptly and stalked out of the room, her hands clenched into tight fists at her sides. She brushed past several priests in the narrow stone corridors, knocking more than a few apprentice priests into the walls as she barreled through the tunnels. She was blind to their presence. All she could see was her father's calm face swimming in front of her eyes, threatening to kill Bakinu. *How dare he…* she fumed. *I hate him. I hate him so much.* She took several turns and soon found herself in an unlit corridor. The sconces on the walls of the larger passageway illuminated part of her tunnel. She leaned against the cool stone and slid to the ground, sitting on the floor in the darkness. She held her head in her hands and closed her eyes, fighting back tears as they threatened to overwhelm her again. Bakinu was locked up, his life in danger. *What can I do? I'm stuck, I can't help Bakinu, I can't stop the Dursturock – I can't even go outside to try. He has me trapped.*

Cara remained hunched over on the floor, a quiet mass of golden-brown hair and dirty tan cloth. People shuffled by in the nearby lighted corridor, unaware of the miserable lump huddled on the floor in the dark. Time passed, but Cara was oblivious.

Hours didn't matter. All she could feel was her father's hatred and anger. His words, wishing she was not his daughter. She thought of her mother, the distant memory of her kind words, the opposite of her father's rigid rules. And she thought of her friends. Trapped. Alone. All that mattered right now was her friends. Leolin, the gentlest soul she had ever met, his life's dream taken away from him because of her actions. Bakinu, locked in a room with guards to keep him from leaving. Bakinu, the one man who could help her now. The one man who understood the truth and was willing to help.

"What would you do now, Bakinu?" she whispered to no one. "They're all wrong. We're the only ones that know the truth. You, me, and Leolin. What should I do?"

She imagined the old man sitting across from her. His tired blue eyes twinkled at her in the dark. *Don't give up,* he seemed to say. *There's still hope.*

"How?" she whispered. "You could die. They'll kill you."

Not if you break me out.

Cara froze. Was it possible? She might be able to get him out of the cave, but what then? The Dursturock was still out there. It would tear them to shreds, surely.

Not if you kill it.

Kill it? By herself? Was that even possible? How do you kill a beast that large? She closed her eyes and imagined the Dursturock, shuddering at the memory. The beast's yellow eyes gleamed over long pointed teeth, a short snout thrusting out from its wide, brutish head. *It was so fast,* she thought desperately. *It ran right after us. We wouldn't stand a chance.* She remembered its hot breath as it lunged at the cave entrance, jaws snapping at her heels. *It was so desperate to get me,* she thought. *So desperate...could that be it? Its weakness? It's hungry enough to follow me anywhere, even into that tiny cave opening. If I can distract it, maybe get it stuck in the cave entrance again, then someone else could kill it from behind. All we need is some sort of weapon...*

She grimaced. Maybe it would work. Maybe it wouldn't. But the alternative was sitting in this cave under her father's hateful glare for fourteen years. Or more likely, starve. The thought of either of these scenarios chilled her to the bone. *I would rather die trying to fight the Dursturock then die in these caves,* she thought grimly. But to kill the Dursturock....to kill such a powerful beast...she paused, lost in thought for a moment, as a plan began to formulate in her mind. Maybe, just maybe...but she needed help. She needed Leolin and Bakinu. Cara stood up suddenly, her jaw clenched in determination, and emerged from the dark corridor, startling an apprentice priest as she swept past him. The young man dropped his bucket and stared after her as she strode toward the main cave, determined to prove her father wrong.

The large cavern was busy with activity. Families were milling around, growing restless at being cooped up in a cave. Several babies were crying, and a dozen younger kids were playing some sort of game involving throwing rocks and hopping on one leg. Cara ignored them all. She slowly walked along the perimeter of the cavern, searching the faces in the crowd for Leolin. A couple priests watched her warily. *Go ahead,* she thought bitterly. *I'm not doing anything wrong, just looking around.* Unless they actually saw her leaving the cavern or breaking Bakinu out, they couldn't report her to the High Priest.

A flash of red caught her eye. Leolin sat on the ground half-way across the cavern, slumped against a wall with his head buried in his arms. His thick dark hair melted into the black obsidian behind him, making his robes look all the brighter. Cara slowly picked her way across the cavern until she reached his side.

"Leolin?" she said hesitantly. Leolin stirred slightly, but didn't look up.

"Leolin," she repeated. "They locked up Bakinu."

"So?" he muttered, his voice muffled by his arms.

She leaned against the wall and sat down next to him, keeping her voice low. "I want to get him out," she whispered. "But I need your help."

"It's over, Cara," Leolin murmured into his elbow, his voice thick with grief.

"No, it's not," Cara replied, her voice urgent. "Just because my father…"

"He fired me!" Leolin snapped, raising his head out of his arms. "You're not my job anymore. I shouldn't even be wearing these robes…" his lower lip trembled and he stopped, blinking back tears.

"This isn't about you or me," Cara growled. "It's not even about Bakinu. It's about the Dursturock. You know it's real. You saw it too."

"So?" Leolin replied. "It doesn't matter anymore. The High Priest said we must wait, and so we must wait. The Penlet says…"

"The Penlet says the Dursturock is unstoppable," Cara said, "but animals can die. I plan on stopping it, but I need help. You and Bakinu are the only ones willing to help me."

"It's suicide," Leolin growled. "Why would I help you die?"

Cara glared at him. "We're all going to die if we stay in these caves. The food shortage, remember?"

Leolin gazed at her for a few minutes, then looked back at the ground. "I can't, Cara. The Dursturock is too strong. I'm useless."

Cara frowned, staring at his defeated frame slumped against the cave wall. Why didn't Leolin understand? This wasn't about right or wrong anymore, or the Creator, or even about his job. This was about life and death, the survival of their people. Whether her father believed her or not, she knew this was the right way, the only way, to keep people safe. And she needed to convince Leolin of this as well. "Look, I know you've had a really tough day, but I need you. My father hasn't put guards on the cave entrance yet, and I don't want to wait to see if he does. I'm breaking Bakinu out of the storage room tonight, and we're going after the Dursturock."

"You can't," Leolin pleaded.

"I can," she countered. "It's either that, or we all die slowly here in these caves."

Leolin eyed her cautiously. "I could tell," he whispered. "All I have to do is tell your father what you're planning."

Cara glared at him. "You won't. And you know why? Because you know I'm right. You've seen the Dursturock. You know it's an animal. And animals can be killed."

Leolin stared at her for a long time, completely silent. Cara sighed and looked back at the rest of the cave. Villagers strolled around, conversing with other families and eating their meager rations for the day. Leolin turned and watched them too, dark brown eyes wide in the dim light. Cara could almost hear him thinking. Finally, he spoke.

"How do you plan on killing it?" he whispered.

Cara grinned. "With weapons," she said quietly. "We know it's hungry. That's our advantage. Remember how it ran right at us? Well, if one of us distracts it by running into the cave, it will probably follow and stick its head in the entrance again. And when that happens we can attack. If you guys are hiding in the grass next to the entrance, you can jump up and stab it. With any luck, that will kill it."

Leolin pondered the idea. "It might work. But I don't know if we're strong enough to hurt it. And where do we get weapons?"

"They have weapons in the storage rooms," Cara said confidently. "We just have to steal some of them."

Leolin swallowed, and looked at his hands nervously. "I…I don't know if I could do it. Kill something."

"Even the Dursturock?" Cara asked incredulously. "The evil force foretold by the Creator to kill us all? Wouldn't your precious Creator want you to protect your people and your home from the end of days?"

Leolin's hands trembled in the firelight. His lips moved slightly as he worried, and then he bit his lip hard enough to draw a small amount of blood. Several moments passed. Cara held her breath, waiting for a sign. Then finally Leolin clenched his fingers into a fist and looked up a Cara, his brown eyes shining in the light.

"Okay. I'll help you. May the Creator forgive me, but I'll help you."

Chapter Nineteen

It wasn't long before night came. A priest returned from the entrance to report that there was no longer sunlight coming into the first half of the passageway. Families yawned and returned to their blankets on the floor. Several priests made the rounds of the room and extinguished many of the lanterns. Within an hour, the entire cavern was completely still. A dim light illuminated only parts of the cavern, with deep shadows extending through the rest. Blankets rose up and down as the villagers breathed deeply in their sleep, and several snores were clearly audible in the silence.

"You awake?" whispered Cara.

"Yes," answered Leolin.

"They took him down here," she whispered. Leolin nodded. They started down the corridor, paying attention to every step in their efforts to stay unnoticed. After a short while, the passageway began to branch. Various narrow pathways and storage rooms loomed at them from the darkness. It was hard to see inside most of them, but Cara could see the vague shapes of blankets and water jugs. Nothing that would help them kill the Dursturock.

"How do you know there are weapons here?" Leolin whispered.

"They had to build these caves from something," Cara answered. "Chipping tools, carving instruments, something. They wouldn't have thrown them all away – I'm sure the cave needs maintenance."

"You want to use tools to kill the Dursturock? I thought you said there were weapons here."

"A tool can be a weapon," she countered.

"Not a very good one," he muttered.

Cara leaned forward into another black hole in the wall, squinting into the darkness. The shapes in this room were different. Could these be the tools?

"I need a light," she whispered urgently.

"But they'll see us!"

"There's no one here right now," Cara said. "We can risk it. Take one from the sconce we just passed."

Leolin obeyed, shuffling off down the corridor where the dimly lit lantern rested on a shelf carved into the wall. He lifted it gently and slowly returned to Cara, his eyes shining in the lantern light. Cara grabbed the lantern and entered the storage room. She smiled at what she saw. Tools! Lots of them, too. Hammers, picks and chisels lined the walls, each lying on a shelf of stone. Larger tools leaned against the wall, their metal tips gleaming in the light from the lanterns.

"Look," Cara whispered loudly, "spears!" She pointed to a long thin shaft of wood. A long flat metal tip with notched sides was mounted to the top, the tip sharp and pointed.

"It's a rasp," corrected Leolin. "A rasp with a very long handle. It's used to remove rock from a surface, in this case from very high places."

Cara shrugged. "Looks like a spear to me. Either way, it's perfect." She stepped forward and picked one up, feeling the weight of the tool in her hand. "This will do nicely." She handed it to Leolin. He held it uncertainly, staring down at the metal tip with a furrowed brow.

"I suppose it's sharp enough," he muttered. "And the handle is plenty long…"

Cara grabbed two more from the wall. She smiled at Leolin. "Now we just need obsidian. Should we just put it in our pockets?"

Leolin shook his head. "I don't want to risk it falling out. It would be safer if we put them on a string around our necks." He looked around the cave, then pointed. "There. The coils of rope."

Cara bent over and picked one up. "This? How will this help?'

Leolin placed his spear and lantern on the ground, then sat down next to the rope. "Hand me a file and a piece of obsidian," he said quietly. Cara hesitated, then obeyed. She grabbed a file from the wall and handed it to him. "There's no loose obsidian here," she said, looking around at the floor.

"Then go find some," responded Leolin, hunched over the rope with the file.

Cara frowned then turned around, exiting the storage room. The tunnel was dark compared to the room. She felt her way down the corridor for a few minutes until she came to another side passageway. This one was rougher, it's walls unpolished. *A promising place to find rock fragments.* After a few minutes of groping around on the floor, she found three finger-sized chunks of obsidian. She cradled them safely in her arms and returned to the storage room.

"Here they are," she whispered. Leolin accepted the rocks. He had already cut the rope into thinner twine-like segments, each piece long and strong looking. He grabbed the end of one of the pieces and began wrapping it deftly around the first chunk of obsidian, forming an x-shaped cradle for the rock to sit in. In less than a minute he had tightly secured the obsidian in the necklace, and tied both ends together. He held up the rock necklace for Cara to examine.

"Will this work?"

Cara nodded, impressed. "Perfect."

Leolin resumed his work. In a matter of minutes, he had three obsidian necklaces ready to go. He handed one to Cara, and put another around his neck. The obsidian lay just over the top of his sternum, glittering black in the lantern light. He put the third in his pocket.

"Now we go get Bakinu," Cara whispered, putting the rock necklace on. The two friends exited the storage room and continued sneaking down the corridor, leaving the lantern behind. Cara grasped one of the long-handled rasps in her hand, and Leolin carried the other two. They traveled for several more minutes. All Cara could hear was the sound of her heart beating in her ears and her shallow breath. Suddenly she heard a loud sigh. She looked back at Leolin.

"Not me," he mouthed, his voice nearly undetectable.

Cara turned the rasp around so that the wooden part was facing forward. She leaned around the corner and squinted at the bright light. A white-robed priest leaned against the wall of the corridor, a brightly shining lantern hanging on the wall just above his head. A dark hole in the wall stood directly in front of him. The priest looked bored. He twiddled his thumbs and stared at the ceiling.

Cara glanced at Leolin. He put up a finger, signaling her to wait, then carefully leaned his rasp against the wall. He straightened his robe then walked out around the corner of the passage, walking confidently towards the priest.

The priest's head snapped around as he heard Leolin's footsteps. He pushed himself off of the wall and glared at Leolin. "What are you doing here?" he said gruffly. "Only full priests are standing guard here."

"I thought you might like a break," Leolin said reassuringly.

The priest frowned, looking more carefully at his face. "Leolin, right?" He shook his head at the red robes. "You shouldn't be wearing those, you aren't an apprentice priest anymore. In fact, you shouldn't be here at all."

"I didn't mean any harm," Leolin said quickly, raising his hands in defense. "I just wanted to help."

He stepped forward and looked down at him menacingly. "You've helped enough already. You almost brought the Dursturock down on us again. Get out of here, before I call for help."

Leolin took a couple steps back. "You don't need to call for help, I'm sorry."

"What are you doing here, anyway?" the priest asked, suspicious. "You know you aren't allowed here." He reached out and shoved Leolin. Leolin flew backwards and fell on his bottom, only a few feet from Cara where she hid behind the bend in the wall, clutching her rasp. "You're in league with the heretic, aren't you? Come to free your friend!" The priest towered over Leolin, looking down at him with angry eyes and raising his arm.

Cara acted quickly, before she quite knew what she was doing. She jabbed the wooden end of the rasp forward with all her might, instinctively moving to protect her friend. The butt of the handle connected with the temple of the priest, sending him flying against the far wall of the passage. She jumped out and brandished her weapon, ready to hit him again, but the priest didn't move. He lay on the ground, completely still, limbs sprawled across the floor.

"You killed him!" gasped Leolin, looking at her in horror.

Cara rushed to the priest's side and felt for a pulse on his neck with her finger. To her relief it still surged strong and steady.

"He's alive," she said. "I think I only knocked him out." A thin trickle of blood fell from his temple, snaking its way through his hair and in front of his ear from a short narrow gash.

Leolin ran a hand through his dark hair. "I didn't want to hurt him," he muttered anxiously. "Creator forgive me."

"I'm sure he will," Cara said, standing up, "as soon as we kill the Dursturock."

"Cara?" a voice called, groggy from sleep.

"Bakinu!" Cara called, keeping her voice low. She rushed forward and peered into the storage room. The room was empty except for the old man. He leaned against the far wall, a blanket wrapped tightly around his shoulders.

"Cara, is that you?" he asked, squinting in the bright light from the lantern.

"Yes," she whispered. "We've come to get you out of here. We're going to fight the Dursturock. We have weapons."

Bakinu slowly stood up, swaying slightly. "Fight the Dursturock? How?"

"With these," she said, brandishing the rasp. "If we can sneak up on it from the side, then we can stab it with these." She looked around the storage room again. "Where's Cheea? She was with you when they took you."

"She's somewhere in the caves," he responded sadly. "I told her to leave. I couldn't be sure what the priests would do to her, and I didn't want you to get into any more trouble."

The old man stepped out of the storage room and into the corridor. The light illuminated his balding head and tired eyes. Cara's eyes widened when she saw his face. A large bruise had formed over his right eye, and a few small cuts drew angry red lines across his cheeks.

"What happened to you?" she gasped.

Bakinu shrugged. "The priests were angry. They let out some of their fear on me."

Leolin joined them. He swallowed nervously and handed Bakinu one of the obsidian necklaces. "Here, put this on."

Bakinu silently pulled the string over his head. He examined Leolin carefully. "I didn't think you had this in you," he said quietly. "Disobeying the High Priest? That goes against everything the Penlet teaches."

Leolin blinked. "The Pelnet also teaches to preserve life and care for others. I am following the Creator's wishes. The High Priest is wrong – he did not see the beast, and has not seen the Creator's true plan. The Dursturock is an animal, and a curse upon this land. If we kill it, then we follow His plan and will save our people."

Bakinu smiled. "Well, whatever reasoning works for you, glad you're here to help."

"Let's go," hissed Cara. "I don't know how long he'll be out for."

Bakinu glanced at the guard on the ground and nodded. The three friends hurried down the corridor, leaving the unconscious priest behind them as they quietly approached the main cavern. Everyone was still asleep. Cara carefully picked her way through the slumbering villagers, following the curve of the wall as it circled around the cavern. At one point, as she stepped over a small child, the blanket shifted and the boy rolled over, murmuring something in his sleep. Cara froze, holding her breath, but the young boy didn't wake up. Cara kept on walking, looking back periodically to check on Leolin and Bakinu. They carefully followed her footsteps, squinting through the shadows to make sure they didn't step on anyone. Finally, they reached the entrance. Cara looked around once more, and then ducked into the passageway. A few minutes later she emerged from the cave, the cool night air slapping her in the face. Leolin and Bakinu stood next to her, gazing over the gently sloping hills. The moon hung low in the sky, half of its face obscured by shadow. The stars lit up the night like thousands of pulsing belknay scattered throughout the atmosphere. Cara shivered. She felt exposed, standing out here in the open. So small, so insignificant, compared to the rest of the world. What chance did they really have tonight? How could she, a lowly little human, possibly stop the Dursturock?

"So, what's the plan?" Bakinu asked.

Cara stood a little straighter, burying her doubts. "I'll be the distraction. I'm going to get its attention by walking around. When it chases me I'll dive into the entrance for cover. It should follow me again, just like this morning, and stick its head in the entrance passageway. That's when you two will attack. You'll hide in the grasses on either side of the entranceway, and when the Dursturock is focused on me I want you to jump out and stab it from the sides."

Bakinu nodded. "Sounds like it could work. There's not much cover, though. We might have to dig a shallow hole."

Leolin walked to the side and kicked his foot around in the grass. "This is a good spot, but we'll definitely have to cover ourselves well. If the Dursturock sees us before it goes for you, we'll be completely exposed."

"Okay then, let's get to work," Cara said confidently.

They all began to dig. Cara joined Bakinu on the left side of the entrance, digging a shallow hole with the tips of their rasps. The sharp metal made short work of the soft soil. The tool rasped against the rocks in the soil, breaking them apart easily. In less than an hour there were two human sized depressions on either side of the cave entrance, both surrounded by tall grasses.

Leolin lay down in one, and Cara and Bakinu stepped back to examine their work.

"It's no good," Bakinu murmured. "I can still see his back."

"Then we'll put something on top of him," Cara said.

Cara and Leolin collected long strands of grass, and Bakinu set to weaving them into a thick sort of mat. Cara looked around nervously as she plucked the grass from the ground, but the night air was completely still. Nothing moved besides the grass as it swayed gently in the breeze. *Where is it?* She thought nervously. *I thought it would have found us by now.*

"This might actually work," Leolin grunted, leaning over to grab another thick piece of grass. "If we *do* kill it…"

"If it comes," she muttered.

Leolin looked around, surveying the hills with alert eyes. "It'll come," he said confidently. "You saw how desperate it was earlier."

"Then where is it?"

"It must be diurnal," Leolin grunted, grabbing another stalk of grass. "Only hunts during the day."

Bakinu finished weaving the mats. They were long and thick, and perfectly covered Leolin when he lay down in the hole again.

"Almost," murmured Bakinu. He uprooted several clumps of grass, root and all, and set them on top of the mat. He stepped back and observed his work. Leolin was invisible. The mat looked like a bald patch of earth, and the tall grass obscured the spot entirely.

"Perfect," Bakinu said, wiping the dirt from his hands.

Cara stepped forward and examined the spot more closely. When she really stared, she could just make out the gleam of Leolin's dark eyes and the tip of the rasp where it lay near his head.

"Try jumping out," she urged. After a few moments Leolin sprang from the hole, the mat flying to the side as he lunged at the entrance to the cave. He thrust his rasp forward into the air, approximating the height of the Dursturock.

Cara clapped, excited. "You got it!" she exclaimed.

Leolin grinned sheepishly. "It'll never see us coming."

Cara glanced at the sky. "It won't be light for a while, but we should be ready just in case. Let's get you guys in position."

It took a while to get the two ready again. Bakinu wanted to practice lunging from the hole too, and so they had to keep on resetting the mat over and over. It was a while before both Leolin and Bakinu lay in their respective holes, completely covered by the mats and clumps of tall grass. Cara stood out in the open between them, directly in front of the entrance. She grasped the handle of her rasp tightly. When the Dursturock stuck its head in the cave entrance, she intended to stab it in the face with the metal tip.

"Cara?" Leolin asked, his voice emerging from the ground.

"What?"

"Can you pray with me?"

Cara frowned. "I don't believe in the Creator, Leolin."

The ground sighed. "I know. But can you still pray with me?"

Cara bit her lip. "My prayers won't make any difference. There's nothing out there, Leolin. No Creator, no omnipotent being, nothing. We're alone out here, and it's up to us to stop the Dursturock. Praying won't help anything."

"Go easy on him," Bakinu spoke up from the other side. "If praying helps him feel better, then let him do it. There's no harm in that."

"How can you believe that, Cara?" Leolin asked quietly. "The Creator is always with us, and protects us."

"Then why did so many people die? Why didn't he protect them?"

Leolin grew silent. "I don't know, Cara. It doesn't make sense. I just don't know."

"Hush, children," Bakinu said. "There's no need to worry. All we need to do is wait. Wait until the morning. And then the Dursturock will come."

Chapter Twenty

The night dragged on. Cara sat on the ground and stared at the horizon, fighting to keep her eyes open. She stifled a yawn and readjusted her legs. She couldn't remember ever wanting dawn to come so badly. She gazed over the fields and watched the tops of the long grasses swaying in the gentle breeze. They were undisturbed by worries or troubles. They had no idea the Dursturock was coming. Cara envied them. The tips of the grass had a tinge of gold that gleamed in the night. *Hang on, gold?* Cara blinked. The grass was definitely shining slightly, reflecting more than just the moonlight. She looked up. A faint smudge of color glowed from the horizon to the east. The sun was rising.

"Hey," she said hoarsely, suddenly wide awake. "Leolin, Bakinu, you guys awake?"

"Yes," responded Bakinu. Leolin didn't answer.

"Leolin!" Cara barked.

"Mmmnn, huh? What?"

"The sun's coming up," Cara said, glaring at the patch of ground where Leolin was hiding. "Are you awake?"

Leolin cleared his throat. "Um, yeah. Wide awake. Do you see anything?"

Cara squinted at the fields. "Nothing yet. I'll walk around a bit. See if I can get its attention."

"Be careful," Bakinu said, an urgent tone to his voice. Cara slowly stood up and shook the stiffness from her legs. She grasped the handle of her rasp and strolled down the hill a bit, staying fairly close to the cave entrance. The sun rose a little higher behind the hills. A few rays peeked out, and the sky became noticeably lighter.

"Nothing yet," she shouted, surveying the grass. A bright flash of light erupted from the sky, blinding Cara for a moment. She blinked rapidly and stepped back towards the cave entrance, suddenly nervous. A low peal of thunder followed the flash.

"Cara?"

"It's coming!" she shouted. A large black mass surged over the hill in front of her. Cara rushed back to the cave entrance and stopped in front of the stony protrusion, eyes carefully leveled at the Dursturock as it raced towards her.

"It's close," she muttered. "And incredibly fast…it's running up the hill. It'll be here in…maybe twenty seconds…"

"TTTTHHHHHHHUUUUUURRROOOOOAAAAAAW WWWWWWRRRRRR!"

The Dursturock roared. The sound ripped through the air and made Cara's hair stand on end, but she stood her ground. The weight of the obsidian on her sternum and the rasp in her hand gave her strength. The Dursturock came closer, huge muscles flexing as it propelled its enormous mass straight at her. Yellow eyes gleamed with hunger, and its jaw hung open to reveal long sharp teeth. It stared straight at Cara, focused on her and her alone. Just before it reached the cave, Cara dove into the entrance, scrambling along the rocky floor to stay out of its reach. The Dursturock tried to follow her in again, thrusting its massive head into the entrance and gnashing its teeth in her direction.

"NOW!" Cara shrieked. "DO IT NOW!"

The beast howled suddenly, its thin black pupils constricting in pain. Cara thrust her rasp at its eyes, but the Dursturock withdrew its head before she could touch it. She jumped out of the cave after it, triumphant.

"Gotcha!" she yelled, brandishing her rasp. The sight before her eyes cut her off, her smile dying from her lips. The Dursturock wasn't dead. It wasn't even seriously injured. Two rasps hung from either side, each tip embedded almost a foot into its sides. The Dursturock didn't seem to notice. It whirled on Leolin and roared again, a trumpet of anger and annoyance. Leolin staggered back and fell on the ground, his eyes wide with fear. The Dursturock stepped towards him, its mouth open and ready to bite him in two.

"NO," Cara yelled. "STOP!" She picked up a rock in her right hand, rasp still in her left, and flung it at the Dursturock. The stone bounced off of the creature's skull, narrowly missing its eye. It spun around, irritated, and lunged at Cara, mouth open and drooling. Cara ducked and closed her eyes, screaming in fright. She heard a roar and a growl, and then felt a long sharp tooth scrape across her back. She screamed again, in pain this time, clutching the shaft of the rasp still in her hands. She winced, waiting for the kill bite, but nothing happened. The beast roared again, but this time the roar was softer and strangled sounding. Almost like it was in pain. Cara tentatively opened one eye and looked up. The Dursturock fell on top of her, its large black neck landing squarely on her back. She grunted and fell to the ground, the breath knocked out of her. She lost her grip on the handle of the rasp. Warm liquid coursed over her neck and shoulders, soaking her clothes. She tried to scream again, but her cry was muffled by the beast and the ground. What was going on? Was she dying? Is this how the Dursturock killed its victims? She stopped screaming, struggling to breathe. A long silence followed.

"Cara!" a voice yelled. She felt hands on her leg, pulling frantically. Another pair of hands joined them. She slid slightly, the Dursturock's weight still pressing down on her. She gasped for air. The warm liquid was all around her, sticky, in her eyes, her hair, her nose. She coughed, feeling it on her tongue. It had a sharp metallic taste. Like blood. Was this the end?

"Pull!" She could recognize Leolin and Bakinu's strained shouts as they heaved again in unison. Another surge and Cara slid out from under the beast, her cheek scraping against the ground. She took in a deep breath of the sweet morning air. All she could see was dirt and grass. Rough hands flipped her over. Leolin and Bakinu's worried faces swam into view above her, haloed by the morning rays of sun as they illuminated the dawn.

"Oh Creator, look at all the blood," sobbed Leolin. "She's dead!"

Cara blinked, confused. *Dead? Is this what being dead felt like?*

"She's alive, Leolin. Look, she's blinking." Bakinu's hands brushed the hair out of her eyes. "Cara, are you okay? Tell me, do you feel any pain? Did the Dursturock bite you?"

Cara coughed up blood, spitting it out of her mouth. She struggled to sit up. Her back burned where the beast's tooth had scraped her, but there were no other sharp pains. Just aches and bruises from the weight of the Dursturock.

"What…" she panted, wiping blood off of her lips. "What happened? What's going on?"

Leolin cried out and jumped forward, hugging her tightly. "You're okay," he moaned. "The Creator have mercy, you're alive."

"Ouch!" yelped Cara. Leolin withdrew quickly. Her chest hurt, a dull sort of ache that throbbed when Leolin touched it.

"You probably have several broken ribs," Bakinu murmured, feeling her over. "Most of the blood isn't yours. It's a miracle, Cara. You're alive."

"Will someone just tell me what's going on!" she yelled, her chest aching from the effort.

Bakinu pointed behind her. "You killed the Dursturock."

Cara turned and stared. The enormous beast lay slumped on the ground, its yellow eyes dull and lifeless. A massive pool of blood pushed out from under it, but it was growing slower now that the beast's heart had stopped. Cara saw the tip of her rasp pointing out of the Dursturock's back, the metal and wooden shaft coated in thick blood where it penetrated directly into its chest. She remembered it lunging at her, the strangled cry of pain.

"It impaled itself," she whispered, stunned. "All I did was hold the rasp…"

"Right through the heart," added Bakinu. "Nothing can survive that. I guess with its magical roar, it's not used to prey fighting back."

Cara shakily pushed herself to her feet. Blood that was not her own dripped from her hair and clothes. She approached the Dursturock cautiously. The thick black skin was caked in blood around the wound. She carefully lay a hand on the beast. Its hide was warm and thick. Muscles as hard as rocks lay just under the skin. She felt the warmth fading away from the body below her.

"It's dead," she whispered. "The Dursturock is dead."

Noises emerged from the entrance of the cave. Pale faces peered out from under the rocky ledge. They gasped when they saw the massive body bleeding out in front of them. Someone shoved their way past the faces and strode out from the cave entrance. The High Priest stood tall, fury on his face, and froze at the scene in front of him. His eyes floated over the dead beast and the rasp sticking out of its back. He looked in awe at the bloody carcass, and then turned to his daughter. She still had her hand on the Dursturock's side, pale fingers contrasting to the thick black hide. She was drenched in dark red blood from head to toe, hardly recognizable through the congealing liquid.

"Wh…what…" the High Priest gasped, his mouth hanging open.

Whispers started emerging from the cave entrance behind him. Villagers began to come out, anxious to see if it was true. Soon there were dozens of people gathered around the dead beast, all wide eyed and stunned at the sight before them. More flooded out from the cave entrance, wrapping around the scene.

Cara looked at her father. "The Dursturock is dead, father," she said, her voice surprisingly strong. She suddenly grinned, fully aware of how she must look at that moment. The High Priest's daughter, drenched in the Dursturock's blood. This would be an image no one would forget.

Several of the villagers gasped and fell to their knees, making the sign of the Creator and swaying in prayer. Most of the villagers looked at her with a mixture of fear and awe.

"The prophet!" one villager exclaimed. "The Creator walks among us!"

A priest threw his arms to the sky. "*For the prophet is one with the Creator,*" he chanted, "*and will come again to defeat the Dursturock and save the land from its wrath.*"

Villagers and priests alike cried out in agreement, and everyone began falling to their knees all around her. Within a few moments, there were over a hundred people kneeling in a circle around her, tears in their eyes, crying out to her and making the sign of the Creator. Nearly the entire village had gathered outside of the cave, and everyone was looking at Cara with a devout expression. Cara watched in amazement. "I'm not a prophet," she said softly, dumbfounded.

"Let it go, Cara," Bakinu murmured from behind her. "Better this than getting in trouble again."

Cara watched in awe as her father slowly fell to his knees in front of her, his white robes now stained by the blood and dirt at his feet. He bowed his head to his daughter and closed his eyes. "I beg your forgiveness, Creator," he intoned. "I did not

215

recognize you in this vessel. I should have heeded your warnings. We thank you for saving us. Praise the Creator and His glory."

Cara blinked in shock. She glanced at Bakinu and Leolin next to her, searching for some sort of normalcy. Bakinu merely smiled, enjoying the scene. Leolin, however, stared at her in disbelief.

"The prophet?" he whispered, gazing at her.

"Yeah," Bakinu snorted, keeping his voice low. "Meet our friend the Creator reborn, daughter to the High Priest and avowed atheist."

"Now what?" hissed Cara.

"Play the part," encouraged Bakinu.

Cara looked nervously at her father, still bent over on his knees. "You may rise," she said firmly, trying to keep the bemusement out of her voice. The High Priest stood, slowly averting his eyes from her face. Her father stood awkwardly before her, and for the first time she saw him not as the over-bearing parent who controlled her every move, but instead as a mere mortal, desperate to help his people and follow the Creator's will. And now here she stood, in the preposterous position of absolute power over her father and her village. How she had dreamed of a moment like this, where others would have to listen and obey her words. But somehow, now finally living this moment, her prior concerns seemed trivial. It wasn't about the Creator, or right or wrong, or who had the power. She just wanted to be free, and to let her village enjoy life again.

She straightened up and spoke up, her voice clear and true. "This land is free," she shouted for everyone to hear. "The

Dursturock is dead. From this day forth we live in peace. Return to your farms and rejoice."

A mighty cheer went up. All the villagers were outside now, a massive crowd of people all crying and celebrating in relief. They soon began to disband, drifting south down the hill towards the village. Families embraced, and many villagers approached Cara to give their thanks and bow in front of her. Several threw themselves onto the bloodied ground in front of her, weeping in the presence of the prophet, and only found the ability to rise and move on when Cara leaned over to help them up. As soon as she touched them they seemed energized, standing up quickly and sobbing their praise, before joining the rest of their group. Cara felt as if she were in a dream, the surreal situation only hitting home when her teacher Mr. Baynor collapsed at her feet and begged for forgiveness, openly weeping as he pawed at her legs. She mumbled a sentence of forgiveness before she dismissed him, and he dragged himself away, shaking from the awe of being in the presence of the Creator. After some time, the villagers had all left, and there were only priests left around the Dursturock. Every one of them remained on their knees, their eyes averted from Cara's small, blood-soaked frame. All except for Leolin, and her father who had still not made eye contact with her.

"What would you have us do, oh Creator," her father murmured, his eyes still averted from hers.

Cara looked over the priests. "Clean up this mess," she commanded, her voice clear. "Then return to the church. I have something to tell you all there." She turned and beckoned to Bakinu and Leolin. Together they left the Dursturock and the priests behind, striding through the gently sloping hills towards the church.

"What are you going to do?" asked Bakinu after they had put some distance between themselves and the priests.

"First, I'm going to take a bath," Cara groaned, flicking some of the congealed blood off of her arms. Bakinu laughed, but Leolin stared at her solemnly, waiting for an answer.

Cara sighed. "I suppose I'll have to tell them the truth. It's a shame, really. I kind of like being worshiped."

"The truth," Leolin whispered. "And what is that?"

Cara laughed. "You tell me, Leolin. Am I the Creator?"

He hesitantly looked into her eyes. After a minute he shook his head slowly. "No, you're not."

"But then the Penlet is wrong," she teased. "The prophet is one with the Creator, and will defeat the Dursturock. I have to be the Creator. I defeated the Dursturock."

Leolin stopped walking. "The Penlet is wrong," he whispered. "The Creator..." he trailed off, unwilling to finish his sentence.

Cara smirked. "...would never pick me as a prophet."

This book would not have been possible if not for the loving support and encouragement from my family and friends. Thank you to all of you.

Jennifer Fyre is a part time novelist with a passion for writing and teaching.